Praise for The Perfect Circle

"A real estate broker finds herself at the center of a house spiraling around family, love, and time in this novel by Italian author Petrucci. A thrilling study of time that playfully intertwines birth and death, motherhood and human extinction."
Kirkus Reviews

"Claudia Petrucci makes climate emergency a literary motif, in a story that spirals, like the interior of the house in the novel, before closing in 'a perfect circle.'"
LORENZA GENTILE, *La Stampa*

"Claudia Petrucci gave the plot of her book a circular pattern. It can be seen in the constant alternation between the two timelines of the novel, which unfolds like concentric circles—a story perfectly told."
Il Corriere della Sera

"It's impossible not to have many questions while reading Petrucci, but she's good at surprising the reader with the answers she gives. *The Perfect Circle* is ready to become a Luca Guadagnino movie, and this is the book you might want to take on vacation to remind you that climate change exists, but that choosing unhappiness over love can have equally devastating consequences."
FRANCESCA PELLAS, *Il Foglio*

"A refined revenge story ... A satisfying novel that keeps you guessing and in suspense until the very end."
Il Piccolo

“Part thriller, part dystopia—a novel as ambiguous as a treasure hunt.”
Elle

•

Praise for The Performance

“All the world’s a stage ... In this English-language debut, Claudia Petrucci provides a fresh take on an age-old issue: the blurred lines between art and life. In the novel, set in Milan, a woman working in a grocery store returns to the acting profession she once loved. She is an incandescent actor but soon suffers a complete breakdown, showing signs of life only when reading scripted scenes. What follows is a tangled Pygmalion story in which her boyfriend and her theater director conspire, each with his own motives, to shape her anew according to their own script.”
The Millions Most Anticipated

“An unsettling and stunning tale ... Petrucci’s captivating character-driven debut explores the boundary between reality and illusion in the theater world.”
Publishers Weekly, starred review

“What’s left of an actor when she leaves the stage? Who is she when she takes off her mask and is no longer just a character? These are some of the questions running through Claudia Petrucci’s debut novel, *The Performance*, and they make for a very intense and original story.”
La Repubblica

"A daring, staggering debut novel."
Elle

"Lush, relentless and fast-paced, *The Performance* is a story that lingers in the mind long after the curtain falls."
Literary Review

"Claudia Petrucci's debut novel is a dazzling story that straddles the line between fiction and reality, between love and possession."
Esquire

"This is a manifestation of talent. *The Performance* is a miracle of perfection."
VERONICA RAIMO, author of *The Girl at the Door*

"Solid architecture, elegant prose, an uncanny story that subtly unsettles the reader. Claudia Petrucci has crafted a wonderful debut novel."
NADIA TERRANOVA, author of *Farewell, Ghosts*

The Perfect Circle

CLAUDIA PETRUCCI

The Perfect Circle

Translated from the Italian
by Anne Milano Appel

WORLD EDITIONS
New York

Published in the USA in 2026 by World Editions NY LLC, New York

World Editions
New York

Published by arrangement with The Italian Literary Agency

Original title Il cerchio perfetto

Questo libro è stato tradotto anche grazie a un contributo del Ministero degli Affari Esteri e della Cooperazione Internazionale Italiano

This book has been translated thanks to a contribution awarded by the Italian Ministry of Foreign Affairs and International Cooperation

Printed by Lightning Source, USA

Library of Congress Cataloging in Publication Data is available

ISBN 978-1-64286-163-1

Company: worldeditions.org
Facebook: @WorldEditionsInternationalPublishing
Instagram: @WorldEdBooks
TikTok: @worldeditions_tok
Twitter: @WorldEdBooks
YouTube: World Editions

1986

On the night of the party, friends around her are drinking, dancing, and celebrating. Lidia is sitting on the floor, fingers digging into the carpet, thinking about the documents. Her friends know nothing about it, they have no idea what he has done. In the papers he sent her was a written waiver relinquishing the property, with a quick squiggle initialed in the margin to represent his signature. She pictures him looking carefully at the page, fingering the pen, gripping it. Lidia is no longer able to share his thoughts. Which is why he disappeared. Lidia has had a lot to drink.

The house is designed so that the sun descends vertically through a skylight before proceeding on its downward course. The column of light passes unobstructed through three floors, down to the circular bowl that occupies the core of the house: a few inches of water filling a silver basin. Staring at it now, for a rather long time, brings the memory of the first day …

Lidia stands up, her body is crumbling, with each movement a piece flakes off and her head floats. She dances, she wants to be happy for just five minutes. That morning, now far off, he said *wait, look here, look, Lidia, in a minute daylight will burst in here, stronger, more wonderful than any other day that came before.* In the center of the pool lies the cornerstone. It is a round, dark pupil, the pleasing detail that everyone sees without noticing. The absolute blackness of the marble is the soul of the eye that is always watching. Down there, buried in the stone, is their secret, and Lidia has no one to tell it to.

She escapes the alcoholic embrace of two friends, one strokes her hair, and has a little green parasol tucked into her cleavage. *Put together two transparent material substances, air and water, and there you have it,* he had said, pointing to the reflections. He had spoken softly, *two transparent material substances.* Lidia slides a hand over her belly at the point where she feels herself vanishing.

The end came quickly, and Lidia realized too late that she had not considered the risk, she had been thoughtless, as her mother would say. But isn't that what love is all about, isn't it about undoing years of not following your instinct, peeling a ripe fruit to the pit and starting over? She closes her eyes. The room is spinning.

She goes to the table, thinks of him forgetting her. Listlessly she rips a page from the contract, tears it diagonally until the signature is torn in two. The sound makes her laugh.

In the kitchen, she finds a folded little blister pack and swallows another tablet. Now the music is ear-splitting, they'll call the police, but who cares—it doesn't matter, she'll have a great time. Nausea. She climbs the stairs that wrap around the inner core of the house in a spiral; on the second floor she staggers to the railing, and laughs again.

On the third floor, Lidia faces the parapet he'd had built of fine-quality wood; clinging to the handrail, she looks down. The cornerstone stares up at her, calls to her, Lidia's head spins. She leans out unintentionally, and suddenly, the half of her that is about to fall is heavier than the one firmly standing on the ground. She plunges twenty-six feet without a scream.

What will be remembered about her is that she was kind and gentle, well-mannered and appreciative—qualities useful for a happy marriage. They will say that the breaking of the engagement was a hiccup along the way, attributable to her recent grief over her father's illness. Since that final day in the hospital, Lidia had become agitated, is that what triggered the death? Along with her will go the truth, the reason why twenty-two years ended in a "tragic accident."

How beautiful Lidia was, what an unfortunate end. What a fabulous house, they will say, such a steep staircase, and everyone will think about Lidia falling over the railing, but no one will be able to really imagine it: what noise does such a slight girl make when she fractures?

Lidia does not have time to close her eyes. She hits the pool squarely, her neck bent at an angle, her gaze fixed on the door. She will lie there watching, a soundless rivulet of blood trickling from her temple. She will lie there waiting, the last day is also the first, with a little patience time will turn back on itself and he will come through that door. He will be as handsome as when she first met him, and anticipating his touch, Lidia will imagine the feel of his hands; he will reach out and say her name. And then he will demolish it all.

Lidia will wait all night, her lips will turn blue and the water black, she will wait forty-two years, forever young, and finally he will return. "Do you know what a cornerstone is, Lidia?" he will say. "The cornerstone, or keystone, is the stone that supports the entire building. Today we will celebrate it. The cornerstone is the foundation." The foundation will go on beating in her dead body like a new heart.

Rome, Monday morning. For the past few hours, the sky has had an impenetrable yellow cast. The toxic cloud drifts up from the parched countryside of some southern province hundreds of miles from the capital, where, for days, a fire has been consuming the remains of a steel mill. According to the experts, the particles will remain trapped in the atmosphere until the next rainfall. The phenomenon gold-plates the cars moving slowly through the traffic.

Riding her Ducati, Irene Sartori, a broker who specializes in estate foreclosures, is traveling through the city on her way to a preliminary visit prior to an auction. Stopped at a traffic light in the shadow of Castel Sant'Angelo, Irene studies the dry bed of the Tiber through the helmet's visor. She tries to predict the clients' possible assessments, certain that this latest ecological catastrophe will be favorable to the sale: foreign buyers often have a voyeuristic fascination with decadence, as long as it is at a distance, situated in an age-old city of art.

Determined to stay on schedule, she avoids a traffic holdup by crossing into an empty bike lane under construction. At the street corner, a team of street sweepers is removing the last carcasses of seagulls poisoned by metallic dust, and this too seems like a fortunate circumstance to her, since the sale comes at the conclusion of an extraordinary street-cleaning campaign. The city administration was immediately alarmed by the risk of an epidemic caused by animal putrefaction, so the sidewalks of the centro are spotless, scoured by jets of water mixed with disinfectant. Just a vague smell of industrial antiseptic lingers, only perceptible outdoors.

When she reaches Via delle Coppelle, Irene rides past clients waiting outside Palazzo Baldassini, and enters the private parking lot, two doors away from the main entrance. Once inside, she takes her tote bag out of the storage container and stows her thermal jacket in it. She retrieves her dress shoes and stores the flats in a cloth sack at the bottom of the bag. As she's checking her makeup in the mirror, her cell phone rings. It's Paolo. Irene would rather talk at some other time, but she's already ignored too many of his calls. When she taps her earpiece to answer, her companion's euphoria is overwhelming: apparently, a week of treatment must be enough to cause his prostatitis flare-up to subside, and Paolo is already asking her if she can stop by his place when her assignment is over.

"I'm running late," Irene says to evade the question, as she's already walking down the corridor that overlooks the building's inner courtyard. Paolo asks her what she's wearing, if she put on the white slacks he's crazy about. Irene pretends to ignore the attempt at intimacy and says goodbye, assuring him that she will do her best to stop by while already knowing that it's not going to happen. She strides across the center of the quadrilateral courtyard and, with the toe of her shoe, rubs at the travertine: two griffins and a full-blown purple rose emerge from the coat of arms. She reaches the entrance, clicks open the lock, and follows the door as it swings inward, opening to visitors two minutes early: "Good morning and welcome to Palazzo Baldassini," she announces, inviting the clients in.

July's chemical heat is bottled up in the loggia, and the buyers' faces are already covered with sweat from waiting. The Russians study the brochures in their hands, while the Chinese and Germans pay no attention to them, hunched over smartphones and virtual prospectuses of the exterior. Irene repeats the welcome greeting in three languages, then brings the simultaneous translator to her mouth: "Palazzo Baldassini is a Renaissance-style residence built between 1516 and 1519. Like all the most celebrated palazzi of the early 16th century, it has a small-scale facade, with only seven windows." She then leads the clients through the cloister in a semicircle, directing their attention from the courtyard to the portico, and from there to pilasters, loggias, walls, triglyphs and metopes, satyrs and grotesques: "In April 2011, a library was built where there was once a garden. The institute that occupied the structure was evicted when state funds dried up, in 2023."

When they climb to the piano nobile, Irene invites the buyers to look at the ceiling and they respond obediently like a platoon, tilting their heads back. "The Giovanni da Udine room is the first known case of integral grotesque decoration in a private palazzo." Some run their fingers over the walls under the eyes of elephants and griffins, while others stroll along the perimeter of the room, hands behind their backs. Still others, particularly the Germans, go on studying the ceiling.

Irene allows silence to fall, to leave room for the clients' imaginations as they trace with their hands, their legs, their eyes, and dream of a world portrayed in films, in books, in stories about the lives that played out in this hall; they fantasize about acquiring privilege to a lost era along with the building stones. Not to mention the projected dinners, coffees, and meetings that will take place in a bona fide historic home, where an authentic Italian past has transpired, and the fancy of seeing themselves strolling serenely along the street in the morning, on an improbably perfect blue-sky day. Irene watches them nourish these illusions or even just indulge their urge to collect: to be able to buy objects, increasingly dubious houses. Then she resumes speaking:

"Decorations of similar inspiration can be found in Castel Sant'Angelo. The room can be assigned to home or office use; a redesignation as a dining room or meeting room is also suggested."

The clients are motivated; in fact, the sale of a multi-story property, at the entrance to Piazza Navona, was guaranteed from the outset. Irene tightens her fingers around the translator. She starts calculating at the foot of the Ceres fresco—how high will the first bid be? She senses the buyers from Jiangsu calculating along with her: three zeros to each of their polite steps.

The ritual Q&A session follows. Irene never stops, she keeps walking, letting the clients jostle along the narrow staircases, trip over one another's questions in an attempt to act quickly, to be the first to get the answer that will enable them to decide. She acts as if the auction were of no concern to her, as if jacking up the price were not important to her and, generally speaking, as if she were there to do them a favor, though always politely.

When the tour is completed and they've returned

to the courtyard, Irene confirms the time of the auction, set for the following day. Suddenly a thud is heard over the buzz of final questions: one of the Russians has collapsed on the marble walkway, and appears to have lost consciousness.

"Christ ..." Irene blurts out, tight-lipped.

Her exclamation is magnified by the microphone, but no one pays any notice. They all step away from the body, except for another Russian and a Chinese client who hunches over the man. Irene follows his lead, reaching out and attempting to rouse the buyer with a smack on the cheek.

"Call an ambulance," she dictates into the microphone, when the Russian barely reacts to the slap the Chinese man has just dealt him. "Easy, go easy," Irene urges him, but he continues undaunted, until the Russian comes to.

Irene communicates with the dispatcher, and as the man begins to mumble a few words, she reassures the rest of the clients. "He's fine," she repeats, "everything's fine." Relieved, the clients regain their smiles, indifferent to the stranger lying at their feet. Some linger for more questions before leaving the palazzo and moving on to an afternoon of visits and appraisals. Irene responds readily, not at all shaken by the incident: this is not the first time something like that has happened. When she goes back to look at the man, he now seems lucid. He stares up at her, vaguely alarmed. Only then does Irene notice the yellow reflections on his skin: on his hand, on his arm too, and on all of them. They're the reflections of a hideous sky.

By the time the ambulance arrives, the Russian appears to have recovered somewhat, even though he can't get up from the ground. The paramedics bundle him onto a stretcher, while one of them asks her a few questions about what happened.

"Will he be all right?" Irene asks.

"A heatstroke. He's of a certain age, isn't he."

"But he must be no more than sixty, give or take."

"Exactly. After fifty, dehydration is always right around the corner."

The paramedic leaves, and the only ones left behind are Irene and the buyer from Jiangsu. The two of them, she and the lingerer, head out in silence, and Irene locks up, swinging the door back on its hinges.

"Arrivederci," the Chinese man says, walking off toward Piazza Navona.

"Arrivederci," she replies.

It's almost noon, and Irene feels the time of day approaching when the onslaught of heat will become unbearable. Before she finds herself caught in the stampede of tourists from the centro, she should head back to the motorcycle, retreat to the office and hide away from Paolo. From Paolo and his urges. What if she went to Francesca's instead? Francesca lives around there. She's the only one who hasn't moved out to the countryside like all her contemporaries on the Roman circuit. Halfway from the parking lot, Irene phones her. "I can't believe it! It's about time!" Francesca says. "Come over right away, before you end up broiled on the sidewalk."

Much of the real estate in Rome that Irene has dealt with in recent years has been located in the neighborhood where Francesca lives, and the only reason she hasn't visited her friend very often are the kids. Francesca and the twins are a single organism: since they were born, it's hard to remember a day when they were not around. To spare them from particulate matter, at least at a tender age, Francesca decided to homeschool them, and as a result she hardly goes out anymore either. They live in an apartment overlooking Piazza Sant'Eustachio. The house, owned by her companion, was the site of numerous parties in their final years of youthful abandon, diversions that for most of those comprising the Roman coterie have never ended, but have merely moved elsewhere—most often to areas in the hills, where the minimum requirements for a decent life, depending on the latest trend, are sustainable agriculture and the right to carry arms. But there's no one among those who retreated to country life that she likes as much as Francesca. The others are fine for weekends, but she's the only one she can really talk with. Francesca's sense of humor, fortunately, has not been lost in the hormonal apocalypse of pregnancy.

Francesca welcomes her to an air-conditioned paradise, not before yet again criticizing her choice of motorcycle travel. She leads her into the living room, where the twins are sitting on the carpet, in a trance, in front of an English-language documentary.

"What are you making them watch?" Irene asks as she sits down.

"A National Geographic marathon, to commemorate the save-the-species campaign. They do it every year," Francesca says, handing her a glass of rose-scented water. "Did you know that fireflies are extinct?"

"I've never seen one in my life," Irene says.

"So, how are you? I can't believe you're here. Tell me what life is like out there."

Irene points to the sky beyond the French doors, and says, "Yellow."

"Oh God, I had almost forgotten, how awful. But I meant your life, how is it going? And work?"

Her life is going well, Irene replies, and her work even better. A real hysteria has broken out, a frenzied hunt for houses. Since the State Cessation decree, buyers have come from all over the world to take part in the sale of historic homes. *For the past two years I've been working too hard*, Irene would like to tell her, but all she says is that working so hard was necessary and she doesn't regret it, especially now that the market has slowed down. The quick deals have gone and only the substantial ones are left, the ones worth taking your time over. The next property she has her eye on, she confesses to her friend, is Villa Pamphili: the auction manager will be selected in less than a year, and she knows someone who could assure her the job.

"One of your churchmen?" Francesca teases her.

"There would definitely be one of those willing to do me that favor, but no, it's not church business. It's someone I've done good work for, who has assigned me unmarketable properties that I've always managed to sell, that's all."

"I'm a little envious."

Francesca glances at the twins, motionless in front of the image of a lioness crouching in the savannah waiting to attack.

"Go on! You're the happiest mother in the universe."

"Yes, I am. But you enjoy yourself. You're the one with the most interesting job, among everyone I know,

I mean, something that doesn't bore you to death when they tell you about it. And then you drive a motorcycle, which is a cool thing, until you kill yourself with it."

"Thanks!"

"And how are things with Paolo? I haven't seen him in ages."

"All right."

Irene sinks into the couch, feeling at home; it's been too long since she's had a permanent place. In the time she's been in Rome, she likes to change places often, and the rest of her adult life is a glossy card filled with five-star hotels, lunches and dinners in restaurants, snacks in bars and highway cafes, constant relocations, and carry-ons. Going in and out of empty houses, taking inventory of furniture, drawing up lists of valuable items; and the buyers, all different, all the same, the formulaic greetings, the questions, the negotiations in Mandarin, in Fuṣḥā, the growled American *rs*, the limp handshake of the British nouveau riche, the staunch solidity of the Ruhr buyers.

"What are you thinking about?" Francesca asks. "How is it going with Paolo? You haven't really answered me."

"That's the third time you've asked me. Great, everything is just fine."

Her friend remains silent, while on the screen the lioness has clawed an antelope.

"So no kids? You don't think about it at all?" Francesca presses.

"Now is not the time."

"But sweetie, you can't put it off indefinitely."

Irene suddenly feels exhausted and remembers the second reason why she doesn't come to see Francesca:

her friend is obsessed with selling her on the idea of becoming a mother, as if she wanted nothing more than to see her pregnant.

"But I don't want them. You didn't want them either, you had them because you were in a bind."

"Yes, that's true ... but don't say it so loudly. They understand everything now."

Francesca turns silent again and together they go on staring at the little round blond heads. The National Geographic special is interrupted by the afternoon news: the environmental emergency continues, no rain is expected for the next two weeks.

"Have you seen the government's campaign?" Francesca asks.

"How could I miss it? It's everywhere!"

"Well, if I were you I would seriously think about it. I'm not saying with Paolo, I'm saying in general. There's lots of funding right now. I know that's not the point, but why have a child gratis? Do you know Adora? They're specialized clinics. By now half the women I know haven't needed a man, to have a child, I mean. Think about it, at least."

Irene says she will think about it, and ends the discussion. Then she says goodbye to Francesca, promising to visit her more often, and certain that it will be at least a year before they see each other again.

Temperatures have begun their descendent parabola and the sky is still stained with the perennial sunset of the past six days. Back in her apartment, Irene focuses on visualizing the next day's auction. She can already see herself closing the deal, an exercise in positive thinking that has by now become a ritual. Then, out of the blue, without anything to prompt her, she finally decides to message Paolo, apologizing for not having been able to see him the day before. A few minutes later, the phone rings, and Irene is sure it's Paolo, who has never understood that a text should only be answered with a text. But it's an unknown number instead. Irene answers the call with earbuds in her ears, and a strange voice surrounds her with a blend of familiarity and vague menace.

"Good evening. Is this Ms. Sartori?"

"Yes it is, who's calling?"

"I am attorney Ferrari. We have not yet had the pleasure of meeting." Irene notes the particulars of the introduction, the tone of voice. The stranger is elderly, he speaks with the urgency of someone who has been awake for several hours. He would like to meet her in Milan to discuss an auction. "I wish to propose a challenge to you: an impossible sale in a very tight time frame. Do you think we could arrange an in-person preliminary interview?"

"This week I have commitments in Rome."

"Very well, what about next week?"

"That could work."

"I would like to send you some information in the meantime, can you confirm your email?"

After saying goodbye, Irene walks back to the foyer and retrieves her laptop. She turns it on, sees the "new email" icon, and as expected, finds what Ferrari had promised to send. She opens the prospectus: the property is located in Milan's centro, but there is no address. She reads the technical specifications without a pause, including those regarding the fee, and scrolls down to the photos. She is immediately struck by the floor plan, which resembles that of a mausoleum, as well as by the shots of furnishings and appointments, somewhat dated, from the 1980s. A regurgitation of bright colors with glass blocks, mosaics, chrome surfaces, marble and leather. The offer is good news, very good news, especially given the potential profit. Then too it's Milan—Milan is home, and right now Irene is longing for home. She could really use a break from Rome.

The cell phone rings again. It's Paolo, but Irene doesn't care to answer because she knows he will do everything he can to dissuade her. He had helped her considerably in the beginning, but he will shower her with advice, recommendations and ideas, with better ways of doing things. He will tell her that, if he were her, he would not be so quick to leave for an interview in Milan. He would act much more cautiously, he would ask the client to discuss the matter further on the phone first. But to Irene, at the moment, Milan seems so pleasantly removed that, if she decided to accept the job, she would spend at least a month there, staying with her parents. Paolo would not be happy about this temporary separation, but at that point he could no longer object, because he knows the business better than she does; he knows that's how it works.

Irene scrolls through the recent phone calls, passing up Paolo's number. She makes a call before giving it too much thought: "Mom, hi. How are you? And Dad?" she asks, walking toward the bathroom. "Listen, I'd like to come and stay up there for a few days. No, everything's okay with Paolo. It's for work. Next week. Yes. That's fine. No, there's no need. I'm forty-two years old, Mom. Yes, me too. See you Monday, but I'll let you know what time. Love you, bye-bye."

When she retires to the bedroom, her cell phone lights up. It's Paolo again, but she doesn't answer. Tomorrow she will tell him that she was so exhausted, she collapsed at nine o'clock. And it won't even be a total lie. She turns on her laptop for the last time, googles "Adora," the artificial insemination clinic her friend Francesca mentioned, and clicks on the first result, launching the home page of the official website. One of the main locations is in Milan. A sign of fate, especially for someone like her who doesn't believe in coincidences. If she accepts the job, she will have plenty of opportunity to inquire directly at the center, to at least discuss it. To find out how these things work, and whether it might make sense to proceed in this direction. She reads the blurb on the website, hoping it will convince her: "*Ethical, fast, safe, affordable: with Adora you can become a mother. Book your first visit at one of our certified clinics.*" It does not convince her but for now, though dubious, she signs up anyway, turns off her laptop and falls asleep with a strange sensation of cosmic harmony.

By the following Monday, Irene is in Milan. It's the day of her appointment with the attorney, and she decides to take the Metro. She spends the minutes waiting on the platform under the misting jets of sanitizing solution, and tries to guess the location of the house Ferrari wants to assign to her. In the train, she focuses for a moment on a boy's hand squeezing a friend's shoulder, the tendons swelling under the firm, youthful skin; even under the yellowish lighting, those wrists, those faces, those necks glow. She's suddenly struck by a realization that makes her rush to the exit at the last minute: everyone seems younger than she is.

Ferrari's office on Via Giulianova, wedged between the Castello and a dead end, is on the third floor of an elegant building. There's no voice response to the video intercom, only the prompt click of the door, then the remnants of a sumptuous, abandoned porter's booth, and dark green carpeting up the stairs. Irene avoids the elevator and walks up to the landing, listening to the soft rhythm of her breathing. She notices the brass plaque—CESARE FERRARI, ATTORNEY AT LAW—before seeing the door, which is partly open. She knocks—no sound from inside, just the grating turn of the hinges. The tall desk presiding over the corridor is unattended; the hall, leading to the sole window, is steeped in blue: blue carpeting and blue wallpaper, with a rhomboidal ochre pattern denoting a vague distinction between wall and floor.

"Ms. Sartori?" the voice comes from back in another room, heralding slowly approaching footsteps. A hand precedes the greeting—*come closer*, it seems to say—and Irene obeys before the attorney makes his appearance.

"Ah, Ms. Sartori, what a pleasure to meet you in person. You are right on time. Pardon my reception but my secretary is in quarantine. They locked down the area from Quinto Romano to Baggio. A new deadly bacterial fever or some such thing."

"Yes, I heard."

"A real inconvenience." Ferrari steps aside, allowing

her to precede him. "But please, let's sit down. Back there to the right."

"Thank you."

Irene obeys, and takes a seat in a Saarinen Tulip chair at the other end of a white marble conference table.

Ferrari has laid out a laptop, hard copies of the documents, and printouts of the floor plans. When he reaches for the fountain pen, his hand trembles, and Irene looks away, but it's already too late—they both noticed it. "Old, but not decrepit," the attorney smiles wryly, gripping the pen determinedly. His face still retains traces of his former good looks: he is, even now, an elegant man, with meticulously styled hair; he wears a tailored suit, and moves sparingly, with the calculation of another generation.

"I should have arranged a showing, but there wasn't time enough." Slipping two fingers into his breast-pocket, he takes out a pair of glasses hidden by a silk handkerchief. "In any case, for the sake of transparency, please know that you were referred to me by Monsignor Vallini."

"An exquisite person," Irene remarks.

"Yes, to be sure. He was very complimentary of your work, describing you as a formidable sales agent."

Ferrari studies her equably for a long moment, and Irene responds to his scrutiny with a comparable one of her own. She can perceive no hint of paternalism, no assessment that she will be forced to counteract; the man has the neutral gaze of someone studying a landscape.

"Now, if you will allow me, I will proceed to tell you about the property," the attorney says at that point, spreading a document out on the desk. "Last July I was appointed receiver to oversee the Kowalski family estate."

The accounts of failed estates are always different and unique, Irene thinks as she listens to the attorney. It's something she has learned in sixteen years of practicing the profession. All rich families are alike; every bankrupt family fails in its own way. The Kowalskis' money had vanished from the family purses as mysteriously as it had been given. The results of mismanagement had wiped out acres of property stretching from the Valle d'Aosta to the French border, along with a yacht moored in Saint Florent, the ritual of events and vacations, personal care, dinners, luncheons, gardens, domestic staff, and the entire ministry of collateral possessions, on wheels, on foundations, and in investments. Wealth had continued making demands on itself until accounts in new and old tax havens were exhausted, eroded at the root, in depreciating assets and growing debt. The hemorrhage had traced a direct path to the principal asset: the house. The first and last legacy of Charles Kowalski, whose suicidal passion for speculation had been surpassed only by the sacrilegious misappropriation of the privilege to which he had been groomed for fifty-six years. The Kowalskis had become penniless for the benefit of prosperous neophytes; the curtain of poverty had lowered on the audience of creditors ready to collect.

"Which brings us therefore to the matter of the house," Ferrari concludes, handing her the bundle of floor plans. "The original house, which was built in 1926, was torn down in the mid-1980s, after which it was rebuilt. An ambitious and—I say this sincerely—rather incomprehensible architectural plan. You will see for yourself. I won't conceal the fact that the sale worries me considerably."

"Why is that?" Irene asks, unrolling the blueprint on the marble tabletop.

"It's a building of no historical value, monumental, poorly situated scenically, exceedingly expensive and, I believe—but you will correct me if I'm wrong—difficult to position. A true real estate suicide mission."

Irene can't help smiling. "You're really trying to convince me that this is an impossible assignment."

"Not at all, I'm certain you will succeed just fine, as you always do." Ferrari folds his hands on his chest, pauses to consider the next thought before sharing it aloud. "Among other things, I would venture to say that a certain amount of bad luck looms over this property. It has had quite a succession of owners in the past forty years. It also seems that, prior to Kowalski, the house was left abandoned for a long period of time, which would have worsened a chronic leakage problem on the third floor."

Irene's finger traces the circular flow of the floor plan, following the outline of what seems to be a huge shaft.

"Nonetheless," Ferrari says, "I don't want to discourage you. The important thing is that the auction be concluded by the end of the year. The creditors are extremely aggressive."

"I don't think that will be a problem."

"I had no doubt. If you agree, I will proceed with handing the keys over today so that you can do an on-site inspection as soon as possible. I would ask that you update me following the inventory. Then we can set up a preliminary meeting prior to the auction. I myself have not yet set foot on the property. I will leave that privilege to you, since I will be buried by liquidation proceedings until at least mid-November."

"Of course."

"Can you get me the particulars of your fee by Monday?"

Already busy rolling up the plans, Irene nods in confirmation, a sign that the attorney must consider equivalent to a signed contract. She senses his body relaxing in his chair for the first time since they sat down. He gives her the rest of the printed documents, directions on how to find the house, then explains how the keys work.

As the meeting ends, Ferrari walks her back down the corridor to the door. "Call me with any questions, I am available at any time," he says as Irene steps out.

Once she's left the office, she recognizes some vague similarities between the attorney and her father, similarities between men of comparable age groups, and a dull melancholy comes over her, a feeling that everything around her is about to vanish.

On Tuesday Irene is ready for the first on-site inspection. Via Saterna is a residential lane between Largo la Foppa and Via Solferino, not far from attorney Ferrari's office. At this hour of the morning, the fog is particularly thick. People inch slowly along the walls of the buildings, hoping not to be struck by some electric vehicle that has ignored the "closed to traffic" sign. In the milky impenetrability, the flickering gleam of fog lights can be seen, signaling approaching passersby; Irene aims her beam upwards, looking for a street sign to confirm the direction. It illuminates the name in reverse, from the end to the beginning: VIA SATERNA. She continues on until her cell phone vibrates, indicating she's reached her destination: the iron bars of the gated enclosure. The gate is unlocked and all it takes is a slight nudge for her to get in. Inside the grounds she can make out the path of the marble driveway, its edges invaded by hordes of weeds, and a few shadowy trees at the sides of the building. Paying scant attention to the facade half-hidden by the fog, she takes the keys Ferrari gave her, each one labeled, out of her pocket.

Once inside, Irene closes the front door behind her and slides open the zipper of her hood, freeing her head. She recognizes the lines of the circular interior design, remembered from the floor plan: her first impression is of an unexpected, monumental, and therefore unwelcoming space, as anticipated earlier by the attorney. The house conveys an image of cold sacrosanctity, and whatever furnishings remain don't help any. The kitchen is hidden by a double wall to the east. The living area retains the yellowish shadows of paintings that once hung on the walls. In addition to a long glass dining table, a display cabinet with crescent-shaped doors, and a pale blue leather sofa, there is an antiquarian reflux of a turn-of-the-century style that survived the furniture removal. The white marble-chip floor is barely visible under a thick layer of grime.

Irene proceeds with the inspection, tossing her bag on the sofa. In the corner, she notices an incongruous element, a can of tuna fish on a low, three-legged table, yet at the moment she doesn't process the information as well as she should, the anomaly of its perfection as well as its presence. Focusing on the walk-through, Irene reaches the open basin in the center of the entrance hall, it too circular. Corresponding to the basin is the circular area of the shaft, open to the roof; a stairway leading to the floors above winds along its interior walls. Irene looks up at the triangular cupola: the huge skylight at the top ensures the passage of light, while the walls enclosing each of the floors are comprised of thousands of glass blocks through which the rooms behind them can be glimpsed: distorted, luminous islands, mottled with speckles and shadows.

Circling the pool, Irene starts up the staircase. The entry archway to the first tier opens onto a landing and comes to a fork: according to the floor plans, walking clockwise through the rooms leads through the master bedroom, the nursery, two walk-in closets, and the master bathroom. Irene mentally notes the required repairs. She flicks on one of the light switches, but the power is obviously turned off. She pauses for a moment to stare at the dark stain of a leak spreading under a window, and tries to imagine potential buyers, to picture the clients and their questions, but she can't get very far, as if needing to see more. She quickly moves on, attributing the dallying to her troubled sleep the night before.

She explores the second floor with renewed energy, continuing to commit details to memory, recording obvious flaws and concerns, and putting off further speculation about a conceivable buyer—someone who might fall in love with a pea-green colored bedroom or brick ceilings. She climbs the last flight of stairs and, once at the top, where the exposed staircase ends, looks down. From that vantage point, the only visible feature is the pool; at the bottom of the basin, the darker outline of what appears to be a round stone can be seen, impossible to notice when on a level with it. A second, inner flight of stairs provides access to a loft space. Irene goes up to a tier that connects to a raised parapet overlooking the open shaft, where the cunning ruse of the circular plan is revealed: the skylight sits on the circular inner wall, while the square illusion of the outer facade is conveyed by the porticos to the east and the terraces to the west, built on an angular plan all around the building's hidden curves.

The space is well lit thanks to the solar exposure, despite the fact that the sky and any landmark beyond the enclosed grounds remain obscured by fog. Here Irene notices something odd: the floor, a parquet with small, dark strips, is clean: there's no trace of the grime that covers the lower floors. Yet for a second time, she defers any explanation and goes on with the job at hand. Resuming her exploration, she comes upon a curving, turquoise wood bookcase along a wall, and some books stacked on a red Swedish throw rug. Piles of stuff are scattered in front of a sofa, and a high-backed armchair faces the stairs. She starts to approach, but this time, what she sees manages to break her hypnotic focus on her work.

Irene makes out a leg sprawled over one of the chair's armrests, the leg of an otherwise hidden individual. Abruptly she can feel the blood pounding in her ears, then her heart hammering in fear. Her instinct is to call the police, but she realizes that she left her cell phone in her bag, three floors down. The body isn't moving. What if it's a corpse?

Careful not to make a sound, Irene backs away toward the staircase, frightened that whoever it is might suddenly turn around, rush toward her, grab her. It might be a thief, a junkie, he might attack her, and no one would hear her cries for help.

Halfway there, her foot lands on a creaky board, producing a loud screech, shattering the silence. Terrified of being discovered, she panics and gives up any attempt to avoid being heard. Dashing down the stairs, running, not looking back, she slips on the last step, bangs her wrist against the wall in an effort to avert her fall, then goes to the sofa and retrieves her bag. When she gets to the door, she throws it open and rushes down the driveway, breathing heavily. Reaching the gate, she closes it with such force that the rusty lock snaps. Only then, safely outside, does she turn to look back at the house.

Whoever it was did not follow her. For a moment, bent over and out of breath, Irene imagines the stranger waiting for her, lurking behind the door. She stands stock-still, watching the doorway, and thinks that the only thing to do is to call the police. She has already started calling when she notices movement at the end of the drive. Someone is opening the door.

Irene instinctively backs away, bumping into the side of a parked car. She sees a shadowy figure materialize in the doorway, moving toward her—the closer it gets, the easier it is to make out its features. It's not a man, but a woman, a girl. Irene stares at her as the stranger reaches the gate and studies her through the bars. Her expression is uneasy, not aggressive.

"Are you from the agency?"

Irene regains her composure, summoned back to reality by the police dispatcher: "Police, what's your emergency? Hello?" She brings the cell phone to her ear, and says, "Excuse me, sorry, I have the wrong number."

When she ends the call, silence falls between her and the unknown young woman.

"Are you here to sell the house?" the girl asks.

Irene recovers her lucidity, shaking off the panic that had mounted during her flight. The girl must be in her early twenties and doesn't appear dangerous. Groggy, a little disheveled, but not menacing; vaguely fearful now, she merely stares at Irene, as if she represented bad news.

"Who are you?" Irene asks her.

"I, uh ... excuse me. I come here to study. I mean, I started coming here to study, sometimes I stay to sleep."

"All right, hold on," Irene raises her hands in a sign of peace. "I'm sorry, I'm sure you have your reasons, but ... you can't stay here. It's illegal. I have to sell this house."

"Yes, I know."

"You know?"

"I mean I thought so ..." the girl wraps her arms around her sweatshirt. "Please, I have an exam at the end of the month. This is the only place I can study. I don't bother anyone, I've never broken anything. In fact, I even keep the place clean, you know? I just have a few books, a couple of things with me—I'm not here permanently."

"No, dear girl, you didn't understand me. You have

to leave," Irene states firmly, approaching the gate. "I have work to do here."

The girl is shorter than Irene, slimmer. Irene studies her through the bars: her hands are clean, her hair washed, her facial skin clear, unblemished.

"I'll leave, I promise. I don't want to bother anyone. All I'm asking for is a little time to make arrangements," the girl says. Getting no reaction, she adds, "I wouldn't get in your way, of course. I could make myself useful, maybe with the cleaning."

"I'm sorry but you have to go," Irene repeats, trying to maintain a level tone. "I have to start my work. You have to leave today." She keeps her eyes on the girl, waiting for a show of hostility that does not come. Eventually, the young woman nods and glances briefly back at the house.

"All right," she says. "I thought as much. I just wanted to make clear that I'm not dangerous, and that I would gladly have helped in exchange for a place to study, before—" A car drives down the street at a crawl, slowed by the fog. "Before finding another place, that's all," the girl finishes, when silence returns.

Only now does Irene notice the bare legs under the men's sweatshirt, the bare feet.

"How much time do I have?" the girl asks.

"How about this," Irene replies. "I have some business to attend to at the recorder's office. How much stuff do you have here?"

"Very little."

"Then take your time, ask a friend who has a car. Get someone to help, okay? I'll be back in the early afternoon."

"All right."

“And please don’t get any ideas, I don’t want to have to call the police again.” Irene pulls her jacket tighter, ready to leave, and the girl looks at her quietly, somewhat crestfallen. “Have a nice day.”

“You too.”

Irene walks away, following the bars of the gated grounds until she reaches the next street corner. When she turns around, the girl is once again an indistinct shadow in the fog.

An hour later, to walk off some tension, Irene decides to go to the registry office on foot, which in any case is located just a few hundred yards away. The route is dotted with distant glimmers of flashlights, and the few passers-by that Irene meets on her way are either people whose heads are covered with hoods or police officers wearing full-face helmets. The streets are silent, and the only vehicle she encounters, crossing at a traffic light along the anti-fog route, is one crumpled against a light pole near a main intersection—an accident that must have happened a few hours ago.

For at least three years, no one has been able to see anything, or hardly anything, in Milan. The “clear” days number at most four or five per month: rare moments in which the fog dissolves and you can get a glimpse of the sky. Exposed to the endless months of scorching Roman sun, Irene always thinks fondly of the Milanese fog: she finds it pleasant, it gives her an agreeable sense of calm. As she continues on to the registry office, she even manages to think of the incident of the squatter as a silly matter that has already been resolved. Her trepidation fades and she again feels excited at the thought of the house, of what she can do with it before selling it.

The registry offices are deserted. Irene avoids the elevator and climbs the marble stairs to the first floor. A clerk returns her greeting from inside his Plexiglas bunker and gives her the pin number to access one of the computers for her search. Irene walks past the desks, vacant except for another woman sitting at the back of the room. As soon as she sits down, she glances at her cell phone, and sees the icon indicating a message from Paolo, then a call from her sister. She ignores them both, and turns on the computer.

To log in, she enters her professional registration number, and accesses the regional land registry database. In the search field, she types "Via Saterna", and the screen returns a three-dimensional map of registered buildings. Irene touches the screen, scrolling through the building numbers, one after the other. On the map, she identifies number 5, a residential condominium that survived the bombings, immediately followed by 9, an austere private villa, recently built. She moves the map until she comes to the gray edges of the unselected field, then goes back, shrinks the map and counts the even numbers, then the odd numbers again. The house numbers continue to jump from number 5 to number 9: 7 seems to have disappeared.

Her phone lights up. Irene taps the earpiece, not taking her eyes off the image of Via Saterna. It's her sister, inviting her to join her for a "sisters day" specifically at a beauty spa. Irene is too focused to object, she sets a date with her and resumes her search. She touches the screen again to zoom in on the map. She magnifies the view until she can distinguish the brass knobs of the condominium entry door and the gray moss on the wall enclosing the private villa. There is nothing where Via Saterna 7 should be except for a curious gray stripe. She presses what turns out to be nothing more than a blank interactive field.

Irene leaves the computer station and retraces her steps to the clerk in the bunker: "Do you have a moment?" she asks, receiving a resigned nod. "I was consulting the registry map, and I found that the property I was looking for does not appear on the register. The house number is not there. There must be a system error."

"Not necessarily," the man replies expressionlessly. "There are other reasons why building numbers don't appear: the property could be under registry review, or the owners could have requested a confidentiality clause due to ongoing legal proceedings, or the property could be unauthorized and therefore not legally recorded in the land register."

"No, that's not possible. I consulted the plans myself, they are documents duly issued by the municipality."

"I don't see how I can help you. I presume you're here for a professional search. Well then, you'll have to contact the owner, it's almost certain to be a registration under review or covered by a confidentiality clause."

"Would you have a listing for properties under review? In Rome—"

"I don't know about Rome, but in Lombardy, no. Regional regulations provide for access to search the documents only once the review has been completed.

For searches covered by a confidentiality clause, as I said, you will have to ask the owner for authorization," the clerk cuts her short with a professional smile. "Is there anything else I can help you with?"

At the end of the futile runaround it is just after eleven thirty, and Irene tries to call Ferrari, but there's no answer. She takes her time, taking a different way back and extending the walk to the Porta Venezia gardens. The fact that Via Saterna doesn't appear on the map doesn't worry her; what makes her nervous is the idea of an irregularity that will nonetheless have to be cleared up and which will at minimum require wasting time. She tries to calm her irritation by exploring the gardens, but soon ends up sitting on a bench, under maples bathed in fog, consulting her electronic agenda. She spends half an hour reviewing the few appointments she's scheduled. The one on Friday stands out: a notation in capital letters of a property at eight thirty. She turns off the screen on the reminder of that appointment, and puts her phone back in her bag. As she looks around her—"around" being just ten steps in every direction before the world morphs into fogged-up glass—she is unexpectedly caught by a distant memory of the gardens. Of the entrance that had been that of the zoo, not far from there, where her father had once taken her as a child to see the elephant. The memory disturbs her, and Irene immediately feels the need to move on again.

She heads towards Via Saterna, despite being well ahead of schedule with respect to her agreement with the girl, determined not to let herself be bothered by the intruder. She walks quickly, intent on shaking off her irritation should the girl still be there—she will tell her that she can't afford to wait that long, that she has work to do, and that she has no time to waste.

When she arrives at 7 Via Saterna, which exists in the real world at least, Irene opens the gate determinedly and strides to the door, which she also opens with a sharp click of the lock. As soon as she is inside, she looks around, and for a moment she fears that the squatter is still there—but there's no one there, not even in the kitchen. She continues her inspection of the house, again up to the third floor, to the attic. There are no traces of the unknown girl, not even a sag in the armchair that must have accommodated her for the night—no books, no dirty glasses, no footprints on the parquet. The only testimony to her stay is a clean floor, where the years of neglect don't seem to have left their mark.

Irene concludes the inspection and returns to the ground floor. Determined to avoid the risk of an unwelcome intrusion, she walks the perimeter of the garden outside, looking for a hidden passage: she immediately finds the open French window at the back of the kitchen, in the laundry room. Before returning to her work, she double-locks the door, and allows herself a sigh of relief. The intruder was merely an unwelcome and short-lived complication.

The next morning, at her parents' house, Irene discovers a bruise on her right wrist, caused by her fall the day before on Via Saterna. She studies the contusion in the bathroom mirror. From that perspective, her old bedroom, framed in the doorway behind her, seems smaller than it is. After her graduation, her mother had removed every trace of her teen years, as she had first with her brother's room and then with her sister's, both transformed into austere rooms for the many guests who followed in succession, at least until arthritis had forced her father to use a walker.

When she returned to Milan, Irene found her father withdrawn in almost complete silence, her mother impeccably well-groomed, still cheerfully unconcerned. Before leaving, she hears them having breakfast downstairs in the living room, and avoids them by using the service door. She decides to go to Via Saterna on the old motorbike she left at her parents' house. Halfway through the trip, a notification of a message from her mother appears on the dashboard screen, which Irene reads only when she reaches her destination: "Shall we have dinner together tonight?" This time, she's able to quickly choose the right key from Ferrari's set—the one for the main door is a single-bit one, with a bronze S engraved on the bow. Irene makes a mental note to have someone come to repair the hinges, which are creaky and resistant. Once inside, she goes to the sofa and puts down her backpack and jacket, already thinking of the inventory. She will have to record everything, every single piece of furniture, fixtures and appliances left there. As she is taking the notepad out of her bag, her phone rings. It's Ferrari.

"Good morning, Ms. Sartori, how are you? How are things going?"

"Very well," Irene replies. "I tried calling you yesterday."

“What time? I don’t think I received any calls. I was in the office all day, until late afternoon.”

“In the morning, around eleven. No problem.” Irene walks around the sofa, settling into a leather chair. A thick puff of dust rises from the cushions, and she quickly gets to her feet, brushing the particles off her pants. “I went to the land registry yesterday. I wanted to take a look at the surveys.”

“Oh, I see, that’s why you were calling me—the surveys aren’t there.”

“Exactly. I’d like to download the three-dimensional plan.”

“The property has been under review by the land registry for a few months,” Ferrari explains. “I was hoping it would be concluded in time for your inspection, but the situation at the regional administration is disastrous, the offices are still a shambles due to the flooding in Varese, some houses have actually disappeared, others have not ... In short, I can’t tell you what a mess it is. We’re all waiting for the approval of revisions that started six or seven months ago.”

“Understood. Too bad, the three-dimensional plan would have been useful, potential buyers always ask for it. Not right away, but I would have liked to start advertising the auction launch through my channels and those of some agencies.”

“It’s not a problem, I can get you one,” the attorney reassures her. “I’m almost certain that there is one that survived the Kowalskis, I remember a very faithful reproduction of the house from the time of the first renovation, in 1985. I’ll send it to you as soon as I find it.”

“Very good, thank you.”

“And the rest? How did the inspection go?”

“Fine. There’s a lot to be done. Today I’ll start the inventory.”

“All right, then I won’t disturb you any further. Call me any time, I’ll make sure to respond promptly.”

“Of course, thank you.”

“Have a good day.”

Hanging up, Irene once again notices the mark left on her wrist: a purple stain radiating like a flower.

1986

He knew that Via Saterna would be a turning point in his professional life. Now that it's happened, Dario realizes that he had foreseen it long before, an awareness concealed by the apparent indecisions and physiological anxiety of planning. In the days following his resignation, he seems to see the coming years unfold before him in rigorous order, already written. The only true determining and unpredictable factor lies in his past: the future exists because it existed the day he met Lidia—she will be forever bound to this specific destiny that will evolve among all possible futures. This specific one, setting aside any other of the innumerable possibilities: of greater glory, of lesser fortune, of modest failure or spectacular ruin. Lidia presented a single future that has engulfed him, making it all the more complex to free himself, break free. This obstructs his ability to reason.

There is still the complication of ownership, the gift that he accepted without thinking. As specified in Lidia's will, Via Saterna is half his. What had she been thinking before giving him such a gift? She'd been thinking of his promises, of course, but which ones? The effort of reconstructing them confuses him, he knows he remembers them all and doesn't want to remember them.

The solution becomes clear one Sunday morning, in the living room of his house, with the children playing and Carla stretched out on the sofa in an imitation of repose; she is nauseous and green. Dario senses his presence as a father grow during the years of his children's development, he looks down on them, pinching their arms, the firstborn's fierce teeth bared, the secondborn's resistance. They are already adults awaiting unhappiness—how could he ever have thought to bring them into the world? When did he make that decision? Why doesn't he remember? Of course he will always be there for them, always and ever, watching over them from a certain distance as his father did with him, never wavering, wavering in private; soon there will be three of them.

On Monday, from his new office, he calls the notary, who drifts off in a sea of chatter, then finally reassures him: *Refuse the co-ownership? Nothing simpler, we'll do a deed, a tiny little deed*, he calls it, he laughs, he's a cheerful idiot, and Dario quickly goes along with it, because the deed must be put together as soon as possible. *But are you really sure, in such a central area, so close to the Castello? Oh, you want to buy outside the city? Oh, you're having a third child, architect, congratulations!* The documents are ready sooner than expected, the inconvenience of a trip to Porta Romana, the signatures, a last conversation with the cheerful idiot, but in the end, they'll see to delivering it, and filing the deed, in a couple of weeks everything will be in order.

Lidia disappears, until a few days after the deed is signed. On a Wednesday morning, Dario spots her waiting outside the office door: he's still far enough away to hide in the crowd of passers-by, until he gets to the opposite side of the street. Having reached the shelter of the porticos, he observes her. It's her, really her, standing with her back to him, planted like a sentry in front of the entrance. How long has she been there? It's almost nine. How did she find out about the new job? A phone call to the old office, a ruse?

Sooner or later she'll have to leave, Dario thinks, no matter how long he has to wait, he'll make up an excuse for the delay, Carla not feeling well. Watching Lidia, he recognizes the imperceptible swaying of her weight as it shifts from one leg to the other, the tension in her stance. She waits for him the way a dog would wait for its master, for him to return, for the abandonment to end: that thought weakens him, he leans against the marble column that conceals him, short of breath. Standing like that, he watches Lidia plead for his appearance, for another half hour, or for an eternity.

In the end, she gives up. She takes two steps toward the door, two steps back, tries to get her bearings, walks away. She walks as if ambushing him at his studio had been her only course. When she is about to go beyond the limit of his gaze and finally free him, Dario follows her. He proceeds in parallel, hidden by the arcades.

The black coat conceals her figure, but Lidia is beautiful, and he wonders if that fact had been the reason. If her beauty had distorted his judgement. Still, she has been so supportive of him, she is so similar to him; she possesses the code needed to translate him. Why was Lidia given the gift of that language, why not his wife?

Lidia keeps walking. On the verge of revealing himself, Dario hesitates and prepares to let her go. As she moves away, he envisions the absence of her voice, of her name, nothing more to experience, nothing to wait for, no more of their conversations, no naivety to be amazed by, no gloating in the pointless advantage of being knowledgeable. Lidia who undoes years of her mother's upbringing by giving in to her tiny negligences, the corner of a nail not cleaned properly, sitting at the dining table with legs spread when there are no others present, the nursery rhymes, a clear judgment in her look, the involuntary provocations, the deliberate ones, her constant devious malice, the hair, the knots at the nape of the neck lazily left behind, to be found, to be untangled.

For the last time, Dario gives in; he follows her for just one more moment. He catches up with her, comes up behind her. Dozens of strangers around him, not a single one who can understand. Her hair is crystalline under the sun. He will never touch her again, he will never look at her again, she is dangerous, she could shatter his life—will she? Now all he would need to do is reach out a hand, caress her, pretend to caress her—she might not even notice. Is there really anything he could regret more than that? He reaches toward her, almost brushes her, hopes she will turn around before he touches her, before he loses his courage, but instead she is far away, in an instant. He will never be able to touch her again.

When she gets back to Via Saterna, Irene immediately heads for the stairs, determined to begin the inventory of the attic. After taking the first step, she looks up and sees what she did not want to see. Feeling a little dizzy, she grabs the handrail. In front of her is the squatter again, leaning over the second floor railing, staring at her and searching for the right words.

"I told you to leave!" Irene speaks first. "What are you still doing here?"

"I'm so sorry, I apologize," the girl says contritely. "I didn't mean to, I didn't know ..."

"How did you get in? You said you would leave! We agreed. I warned you that I would call the police." Irene puts a hand on her earpiece.

"Wait, please," the girl says. "Let me explain. I did leave, I tried to find a place. But there's nothing, there's no place where I can stay and study. I tried at the station, but yesterday it was too cold, and ... please, let me explain. Can we just talk for a minute?"

Irene heaves a sigh of frustration. "Come down," she orders, backing away towards the central pool.

The intruder hurries to obey, still wrapped in her sweatshirt. She looks guilty and seems frightened, as if Irene's incursion had scared her to death.

"How much do you want?" Irene asks her. "What will it take to make you leave?"

The girl widens her eyes, very nearly offended. "But I don't want money!"

"Look, I'm here to do my job," Irene persists. "I have to sell this house, and I can't do it with you underfoot. I can't sell a house with a squatter in it, do you understand?"

The girl shakes her head. "Listen to me, I'm only here because I need a place to study. If I can't study, I can't take my exams, and if I can't take my exams, I can't graduate, and if I don't graduate, I'll never be able to get back to a normal life."

"Is it possible that you don't have another place to stay, a friend?"

The girl avoids her gaze. "They've all gone away. Believe me, I want to leave, I would leave right now if I could ... but I need some time. Look, in a few weeks a place should become available. My intention has always been to go and leave everything in order, understand? I don't want to bother anyone!" the girl shouts, taking two steps forward, rolling up the sleeves of her sweatshirt and baring her thin arms for Irene to check. "See? I'm not a drug addict, I've never smoked a joint in my life. I just had a bit of bad luck. And then I found a quiet place to study, and I stayed here. But very soon I'll have my room at the hostel, I've been waiting a year and there are only a few weeks left to go. I don't have any friends here, I don't have anyone. I can't sleep in the station or out in the street, please ..."

Irene crosses her arms, and remains silent.

"Last night, I came back and started cleaning the bathroom, the one on the third floor. So that today you'd see that if you let me stay here, just for a little while, I can make myself useful."

The squatter seems sincere, and her eyes are teary—her fear seems genuine. Irene thinks of herself in her twenties, of the university semesters spent at her parents' house, when the fog in Milan was still a winter vagary. The distance between her and the stranger seems enormous, unbridgeable, and she feels the tension of fear easing.

"How did you get in?" she asks again.

"From the back. I have the key to the laundry room," she admits. "I found it when I got here, and it seemed unwise to leave it in the same place yesterday."

"Give it to me."

After a moment's hesitation, the girl slips her hands behind her neck and unties the knot on a thin cord. Reaching out, she hands Irene the key secured to the cord. Irene takes the key and puts it in her pocket.

"I know you're going to tell me that I have to leave now, but I thought about it, and I wanted to explain a few things to you. I'm a good person, and—"

"Okay, okay, listen," Irene interrupts, exasperated. "I don't have time to discuss this right now. I have to talk to the client about it."

"Sure, I apologize," the girl says submissively.

Irene looks at her and tries to imagine her sleeping in the station at night. She seems unsuited to life on the streets, so thin and well-groomed. For a moment she wonders how someone with the face of a schoolgirl could end up here, begging for a place to sleep.

"Can you show me this bathroom?"

The girl lights up and nods. "Of course."

Irene gestures for her to precede her up the stairs, and follows behind, keeping an eye on her. By now she is almost certain that she is not a danger, but she still feels the need to remain alert.

When they reach the third floor, she notices her bare

feet: the girl walks around the house without shoes. When they come to the bathroom, the intruder leads the way, opening the window to make sure her work can be seen. Irene examines the floor. The purple tiles have been cleaned, the grout scrubbed, the sink and toilet fixtures polished. Even the mirror shines, despite the residual rust stains. The girl leans over the Jacuzzi; the brown stain has been washed away, and with a fingernail she scrapes the invisible residue, leaving her bare foot covered in white dust.

"There are some cleaning products, down in the kitchen. The mirror might need replacing, the grime won't come off."

Irene looks around, maintaining a neutral expression. "Have you already been to the cellar?"

"No."

"Let's go down."

She steps aside to let her go first again, and this time it seems like the idea makes the girl nervous. Irene watches her carefully as she goes down the stairs, a few feet in front of her, down to the ground floor. She leads her to the kitchen—according to the floorplan, the access to the stairs to the basement is in back, hidden by a closed door. She retrieves Ferrari's keys from her bag and starts reading the labels.

"I tried to take a look, a while ago, but the door was closed and I wasn't dying to go and see," the girl says, leaning against the wall.

Irene doesn't look at her, but she recognizes a note of childish fear in her voice at the thought of what might be lurking in the cellar.

"I'm not sure this is the right one," she says, trying to choose one from the bunch. She tries all the keys, but none of them work. “Okay,” she says, giving up. “Let’s go back inside.”

The girl observes the protocol, walking ahead of her. In the living room, Irene tries to call Ferrari. Again, no answer.

“Okay, I have to get these keys,” she says. “And I have to call the client. I’ll call the client, get the keys, and come back.”

“All right.”

“In the meantime, don’t get any funny ideas. You can stay here until I get back, but if anything happens, I’ll call the police, okay?”

“Okay.” The girl smiles. “Thank you.”

Irene pretends she hasn’t heard. Ending the conversation, she zips up her jacket, puts on her helmet, and heads for the door.

“I’ll wait for you then,” the girl says. “Anyway, I’m Lidia.” Irene nods and doesn’t respond, closing the door behind her.

Ferrari doesn’t answer the phone, nor does he call her back. In the early afternoon, Irene tries dropping by the office, but the intercom remains silent and the reception area is still deserted. She goes back to her parents’ house feeling like she has spent another inconclusive day and finds her mother in the kitchen, supervising the housekeeper as she prepares dinner.

“I don’t understand your brother,” she says as soon as Irene sits down at the counter. “Get down from there. I swear your brother is a mystery. When did you last hear from him? Did you hear about that new one of his? He can’t stop talking about her. But tell me, what on earth was wrong with Lory? She's always been patient with him."

Her mother leans over the pot, pauses to smell the sauce, and resumes her analysis of Irene's brother's ex, yet another in a long line of excellent girls, from excellent families, whose every single quality her mother would be able to name, one by one, girls who then became young women or mothers of young women. For thirty years, her brother has been fishing in the same pond, a fixation that Irene has never understood, which in fact he has in common with their sister, Elena, both of whom have always chosen partners with whom they share the same understanding of reality. Irene pretends to listen. She feels utterly removed from the idea of belonging generated by similar or common experiences, sometimes identical—the same schools, the same parties, the same riding lessons, the same periodic ethical revolutions, the conversions to environmental policies, the generational recitals of renunciation of privilege. The gap that separated her from the birth of her older siblings has always seemed to her an insurmountable obstacle to achieving a sense of affinity. She grew up without the challenge of a model or commonality, and she left it all behind as soon as she finished university, with no traumatic rupture: if she thinks about it, she feels as though she had a lot of fun and then went on to have a good time elsewhere.

As her mother talks, Irene keeps an eye on her cell phone, hoping for a call from Ferrari; instead, Paolo writes to her, an "I miss you" that is impervious to her lack of responses of the last few days. Just before her mother announces that dinner is ready, the reminder for the following morning's appointment at the clinic arrives. Irene covers the screen with one hand when her mother approaches. "You're really something, you are," she says. "Go sit down, your father has been at the table for half an hour."

At dinner, her mother asks her about work, about Rome, and at the other end of the table her father participates by nodding, following the turns of the conversation with an "ah, I see" or an "oh." Her mother doesn't dwell on Paolo, which suggests to Irene that the sudden trip to Milan has made her suspicious. She is certain that, given her romantic situation, her mother has been talking about her for years as if she were the real unknown in the family, in the same exact terms in which she talks to her about Ettore and to Ettore about Elena, pretending to be unaware of the fact that her children also communicate with one another.

"So work is going well," her mother concludes over a sorbet at the end of the meal.

"Yes, pretty well," Irene replies. "I've been working on properties in Rome lately, occasionally some traveling, but mainly focusing on Rome. In the last few months, I've managed the sale of five historic homes and as many private residences ... I don't think I've ever worked at such a pace."

"And the house here in Milan?" Her mother rests her chin on one hand, looking at her eagerly. "You haven't told me anything about it yet."

"It's very odd. Square on the outside and circular on the inside."

"How do you mean? I don't understand."

"The exterior looks like a normal square-shaped

house, but the interior is round. An idea that they could only have come up with in the eighties. It's very spacious, on three floors, with a gigantic skylight."

"Imagine that," her mother exclaims, smiling. "I've never seen anything like that. You, dear?"

Her father's reply is to drain his glass.

"I'm only just starting and there's the inventory to compile, all the furniture to be restored, but I'm sure I'll be able to sell it at auction at an insane price."

Irene can't restrain her enthusiasm. The idea of a sale still excites her, after all these years, and she can't help but think about the day of the inspection visits, mentally drafting the words that she will cram into them. She thinks about the money, always, about the percentages: she plays with projections, the possibility of accruing drives her. She feels that a drop or two of wine will help her hide her agitation, but when she reaches out, her hand knocks over the glass, spilling the wine on the tablecloth. She senses her father's eyes fixed on her.

Her mother tells her not to worry, smiles, dabs at the stain with a napkin. "You're just like you were when you were three, a tornado."

"Sorry, Mary," Irene says to the housekeeper, when the woman comes to clear the table.

"So, where is this house?" her mother asks, passing the cutlery to Mary.

"Zona Castello, on Via Saterna."

Irene strokes the wood finish on the table, a piece her father had sent from New Zealand when she was still a child.

"Never heard of it, but that area is full of little streets you never go to unless there's a reason," her mother says. "I'm really proud of you."

She squeezes Irene's arm, caresses it with the side of her thumb.

"Right, dear?" her mother adds, seeking her husband's eyes.

Irene glares at her, gently pulling away. Her mother is always trying to make things between her and her father work better than they have in the last forty years. She can't accept the idea that the two of them, so similar on the outside—the same green eyes, the same willfulness—are not made to be friends. Besides, her father has never been anyone's friend, a fact that Irene came to terms with very early on, maybe at twelve or thirteen.

"And are you happy?" he asks tonelessly.

He observes her. He studies her the way she has sensed him studying her work over the years: questioning, weighing. Gradually, she has stopped wondering what the question is, that one question that her father has always asked himself when scrutinizing her.

"Yes, I am," she replies with a calm smile.

Her father nods, remains silent, plants his elbows, clasps his hands in front of his chest and rubs them together; he looks away, then turns to her again.

"I really will never understand—" he says, unexpectedly.

"Dear—" her mother tries to interrupt him.

"It's truly still a mystery to me," her father continues. "I swear, it's a thought that almost always leaves me appalled, more often completely disheartened. Years of architectural studies, we paid for your college, introduced you to the right people, all the right people, for the purpose of assuring you a vaguely meaningful life, a minimal push toward a noble goal ... and you decided to become a salvage dealer."

He stops, waiting, but Irene doesn't react.

"I think you're exaggerating," her mother raises her voice.

Her father ignores her, continuing to stare at Irene, searching for a clue to the enigma.

"You're unshakable," he tells her.

"I am," Irene replies.

"I'd like to understand what makes you so gratified, so proud of your work."

"I'm good at it, and honest. They come to me because I'm dependable," Irene says. "Like you."

Her father scowls disgustedly. "I'm sorry, but you can't make that comparison. I've always had ethics. Your ethics respond to criteria far removed from mine, and unlike mine, they are despicable. The country is going to hell, there's nothing left. The properties you sell to the highest bidder don't belong to individuals, but to history, to the past, to a past that is also yours. Houses are not objects, they've been homes for human beings. They are plans conceived with lofty notions, often with feeling ... concepts of construction, of edification. And you take these ideas and sell them to someone and deny them forever to someone else. Historic homes that become hotels, public museums transformed into private homes, rich people who shower under Raphael's frescoes. It's pure madness."

Irene doesn't flinch. Her father's face is mottled, stains under the skin like washes of watercolor. Now he's no longer looking at her but at his plate, chasing a sequence of thoughts inaccessible to anyone else. There is nothing new in what he has just said: as he gets older, the same judgments Irene heard about herself as a girl are repeated, though formulated more deftly now, increasingly caustic. With each passing year, her father is ever more clearly aware of what has made him so dissatisfied with her.

"It would happen in any case," Irene remarks coolly. "Even without me."

Her father clutches the white napkin as if he were going to strangle it and goes back to scrutinizing her in silence.

"Someone else would sell these properties instead of me, and it wouldn't make any difference," Irene adds, meeting his eyes. "All I did was adapt to a state of affairs that is irreversible, over which I had no control."

"There is a substantial difference," her father says.

"I don't agree," Irene replies. "If we really want to play the blame game, we should make it a generational issue, and if we make it a generational issue, your generation will always be infinitely more culpable than mine."

Her father allows himself a sardonic smirk. "It's not a competition."

"Of course. I'm just trying to live my life, like all the others, and live it to the best of my ability."

"I can tell you from personal experience that you will regret those words, you will regret what you thought, what you did and what you didn't do, and at the end of your life, just as at the end of mine, all those decisions made with the idea of being better off, of working for your own gain, will seem melodramatic and irreparable."

Her mother heaves a sigh and shakes her head. They

both remain silent as her father struggles to push his chair back, gets up from the table with the help of his walker, and moves away one uncertain step at a time, disappearing into the living room.

Irene searches within herself for any bitterness, even a trace, but all she finds are vague memories of an early, distant, elusive hurt. She has tried for a long time to evoke it—she tried with meditation, then with a course of analysis that proved useless. Even Paolo, one of the few people with whom she has discussed her dissociation, came to describe her inability to grasp the extent to which her father's rejection must have wounded her as "strange".

"His illness is making him more unkind," her mother says, looking at her worriedly. "He's not angry at you."

Irene smiles at her, caressing the hand that held hers tightly throughout the conversation.

"I know," she lies. "Don't worry."

Her mother is about to say something, when Irene's cell phone rings.

"Work," Irene says, touching her earpiece.

Her mother smiles. Irene has the feeling that she goes on looking at her even when she turns her back and steps out onto the balcony.

"Good evening, Ms. Sartori," Ferrari says at the other end of the line.

"Good evening."

"Please excuse me, I took the day off today for a medical visit. I've called you back as soon as I could."

"No problem," Irene says. "Just a couple of annoying situations."

"Tell me."

“I couldn’t find the key to the cellar,” Irene explains.

“That’s strange, I was sure I’d given you the whole set. Did you try the one with the green label?”

“Yes,” Irene says. “All of them, including that one. I need to get into the cellar as soon as possible to start the inventory.”

“Of course. I’m really sorry for the inconvenience. I’ll have my copy left in your mailbox early tomorrow morning. That way you can start work right away.”

“That would be perfect. Thank you very much.”

“The key to the mailbox is the one with the yellow label.”

“Excellent.”

“And the other troublesome matter?”

Irene looks down from the balcony. Along the street, the fog drifts low in irregular patches under the lights of the street lamps. “I thought I had solved it, but yesterday the disturbance, let’s say, showed up again. And I wanted to ask for your advice.”

“Sartori, you’re worrying me.”

“No, no need to worry, nothing that can’t be remedied,” Irene reassures him. “But there’s someone living in the house.”

Ferrari is silent for a few seconds. “That’s not possible, on-site inspections were done.”

“When was the last one?”

“Three months ago.”

“So the girl must have entered the house after the inspections.”

“The girl?” Ferrari interrupts. “So the house is occupied?”

“I wouldn’t say occupied, the girl is harmless,” Irene explains. “From what she says, she got in through the back door, from the garden. She's not a drug addict; I'm sure she's a decent person experiencing a difficult time. She was looking for a place to stay. She's waiting for a room in a university housing facility, or something like that."

"But you should have told me right away," Ferrari says, agitated. "I'll send someone to throw her out immediately."

"I don't think that's necessary, I can take care of it. I ordered her to leave two days ago, but yesterday she came back. She's harmless, as I told you, she hasn't damaged the property or shown any aggressive behavior. I just wanted to let you know."

"That's not the point, we can't afford to have a young girl underfoot," Ferrari cuts her short. "If she's still there tomorrow, call the police."

"I can convince her to leave, there won't be any need to call the police".

"Yes, I'm certain of it, but if the need arises, don't hesitate. Sartori, listen to me: Milan is full of young people living on the edge, they're camping everywhere. At best she's a squatter, and you certainly don't need me to explain to you why she needs to be thrown out as soon as possible."

"No qualms about it, believe me," says Irene, trying hard to hide her irritation. It irks her that the attorney thinks she's such a soft touch. "I'll resolve the matter tomorrow, I just wanted to inform you."

"You did well." Another cough. "It's unacceptable. We can no longer let our guard down. You'll see, the progressives are right to want to build the wall."

"The wall?"

"Yes, you don't know? There was a huge brouhaha

at city hall last month. How did you miss that? The progressives are proposing the construction of a wall that would divide West Milan from East Milan, to better manage the pockets of crime. After all, you hear these kinds of stories and you wonder."

"A wall?" Irene asks again, bewildered.

"Yes, a border wall," Ferrari says. "Besides, we're not the only ones, the proposal follows a European trend—what am I saying, a global one. Look at Copenhagen or Helsinki, they've already started building. There are too many of us in the cities, Sartori. Anyway, keep me updated on this squatter. Tomorrow morning you'll find the keys to the cellar in your mailbox."

"Perfect. I'll be in touch tomorrow."

Ending the call, Irene lingers on the balcony for a few more minutes, in the evening's muffled silence. Only by listening intently can the echo of sirens be heard far off in the distance.

1986

In the days following the evening of the confession in Via Saterna, Dario's love for Lidia becomes viscous, loathing spreads quickly, details unravel—a kneecap, the corner of a mouth. Dario's memory becomes more and more precise: justifying the potential devastation of his family with two centimeters by two, ten centimeters by five, eight centimeters by four, a millimeter of epidermal depth if we want to be generous: a madness ready to become confused and distant, if it weren't for ...

They contact him on a Wednesday evening at dinner time, the phone rings and Dario answers before Carla. Something like that wouldn't be like Lidia. Still, the sound of the formal, male voice is a relief. They're calling from a large studio in the center, one of those with a name that you already start to dream about in your head in your first or second year of architecture, to fantasize about without even knowing why: everyone thinks about it, so you do, too. They invite him to an informal interview, yes, the architect himself, he asked about you, coffee, the day after tomorrow, yes, San Babila, the studio is still there.

When he comes back to the table, Carla doesn't ask questions. She's lost weight, she's tired, yet she always speaks to the children with her usual level tone. Even now that she doesn't move much, she speaks to them as if her anemic arms were embodied in the strong arms of the housekeeper. The housekeeper they have already had to hire and cannot yet afford, but who they will perhaps be able to afford soon. An interview the day after tomorrow, an important firm, Carla smiles weakly, then leans forward from her chair and arranges some ferns in the vase while the children explode in screams of hysterical wonder. Carla, dear, Carla ...

An organic issue with glucose management, that's what the doctor says: very high probability of miscarriage, yet his wife clings to the fetus that clings to her; in mutual agreement, they proceed to turn the host body inside out, outside in, and both cling to him, sucking him into the vortex. Lidia also clings to him, and with her, the house, the project, the guilt.

Two days later, Dario finds himself sitting in the meeting room that obsessed his freshman dreams, in a storm of existential bile that threatens to submerge him, while the architect sits erect in the chair in front of him, looking somewhat like a bank clerk.

"The plan is amazing," the architect says, leafing through the first of the series of exteriors of Via Saterna. "Daring," another angle, "experimental," his mouth speaks but his face remains motionless: this man is an anatomical prodigy lent to the construction world. "There's Loos, Behrens, an obeisance to Palladio, it shouldn't work under any circumstances, and yet it works, it works." For the entire duration of the informal interview, there is nothing but work talk, barely a minute devoted to the coffee, boiling hot, which the architect swallows in one gulp. Dario burns his tongue trying to drink it, but the proposal arrives promptly and there is no time to feel pain.

He accepts the new job with no qualms about his

loyalty to his superior, the boss who first belittled and obstructed his project for Via Saterna, and then, too late, took credit for its success, with insufficient enthusiasm to compensate for the initial threats of dismissal. No one would listen to him at the time, no one, all anyone in his office thought about was pleasing the client. *But the client must not be pleased*, Dario would like to say out loud, the client, he's sure of it, the client, the owner, must be displeased, opposed, treated with contempt when necessary, always squashed, especially if he actively exercises his ignorance by digging in his heels for the ugly, or worse, for the banal. That's the way it was with Via Saterna: Lidia's fiancé, his dreary idea of a family residence, as if it were necessary to apply such degradation, such indignity to the distribution of spaces in a home.

Loos, Behrens, Palladio, the Villa Rotonda, but also and above all the disturbing origin of the project—how to explain it? The only truth, the most acceptable, is that the Via Saterna project did not exist before his meeting with Lidia, and was only afterwards, in the moment immediately following, tainted by its genesis.

Perhaps Lidia had believed in him because she had seen herself depicted two-dimensionally: a house that looks like a square on the outside and is a circle on the inside. The Via Saterna project is based on that deception, on the assurance of a certain presumption in the eye of an onlooker and the subsequent unmasking of preconception, the crumbling of logical deduction. Lidia wanted to be able to see herself constructed. Palladio, or rather God, a spiritual deviation, as well as Ledoux's House of Pleasure, the cells arranged in three circular spirals in a monastery of Trappist monks built in Belgium in 1909, the Towers of Silence of the Zoroastrian cult, Bentham's panopticon. The panopticon, the eye that always watches ...

So he recognizes every step, every idea that came as a manifestation of an external will, every architectural reference matured a posteriori, when by then everything was finished, every detail as an evil plan that has him as victim, a surreal, malevolent coincidence. Someone must have drawn on his resources, dipped their hands into his skills, extracted them, and applied them to the design. Dario clearly remembers the foundations of Via Saterna at the moment of demolition. He wishes he could control time and stop before the mistake.

He thinks of Lidia, imagines seeing Via Saterna the way he saw her: that rounded head of hers, a perfect circle that can be intuited under the black hair, the smooth forehead. Though Lidia's beauty is serene and pure and almost innocuous, he always wants to desecrate it, to cover that head with his hands, tighten them around the perfect circle, press it until it breaks, always the urge to keep at bay, to abuse her until he wears her out. Lidia raises her eyes to him, the pupils floating on two milky crescents: a long needle is all it would take to puncture a pupil and penetrate the gray matter—so horrific is the desire, so difficult to temper. In Lidia's gaze a consummate love persists. To consume her in that feeling, to flay her, to be reclaimed in the attempt, that's what it was; ultimately to reconstruct a mind worthy of judging him.

The house looks at him: Lidia looks at him, sadly, immense.

The cold has arrived. Dario slows down, then loses his courage at the intersection, deterred by a pair of approaching headlights. At the gate, the house looks at him, inside Lidia is sitting on the sofa. She greets him, welcomes him in, these are the days meant to expect good news, and she waits, calmly. Once he enters, she performs the role she is still learning, the role of lady of the house: she takes two shiny glasses, fills them with wine, makes conversation, and Dario becomes two people as he hears himself answering. She has small hands, and he has forced her to live alone: it is impossible to cleanse himself.

He asks her to leave the glasses on the table for a moment. He tells her exactly what he imagined he would say, in the way he imagined he would say it: "I have to talk to you." No hesitation. He sees Lidia's foreboding. "I am truly saddened by what I have to tell you," he begins. But Carla is expecting a child, our third, it wasn't supposed to happen, it was an accident, a truly incredible disaster, she is ill, she might need to remain confined to bed for many months, that evening I didn't want to arouse suspicion, she had asked me if there was someone else, I wanted to protect you, you hadn't broken off the engagement yet, it was an inexcusable error, yet I hope that one day you will be able to forgive me, your forgiveness is everything to me, but Carla is too ill, I can't leave her, given the circumstances we can't continue seeing each other, you see that, too, don't you? Carla is risking a great deal and wants the child at all costs, I can't abandon my family right now, but I will always be there for you, I swear on what is dearest to me, I will always be there for you, you know, Lidia? but now it would be a crime, I need time, you need time too, you're so young, I'm terrified, this is not goodbye, can you have mercy on me? do you love me? can you forgive me?

Lidia's pity has the wrong face, contracted, she absorbs the news, a possibility already considered, already formulated. When Dario tries to take her hand, she pulls it away brusquely. She refuses to look at him, responds with silence to Dario's new attempts, to his plea that she say something.

The appointment for the preliminary meeting at the clinic is online, at nine fifteen on a Tuesday. Irene leaves her parents' house very early, drives to a conference facility in the center, and at an exorbitant price rents a cubicle overlooking the only window. Through the glass, she can see her motorcycle parked along the avenue, and farther away, a faded view of the surroundings of Piazza Castello; the fountain shoots out neon-blue jets, fluid projections of water.

Irene accesses her profile from station five, and the appointment reminder appears on the screen, a notice that immediately triggers a countdown. She watches the numbers reel backwards, her mind a flat, blank surface. She slept badly; she had strange dreams of floods, and her father may have been in one of them.

At nine fourteen, a welcome video opens on the desktop with new age music in the background. Irene takes out her earphones and puts them on the desk: images of attractive forty-year-olds scroll by on the monitor, gorgeous women running in sunlit parks, chairing meetings against metropolitan skylines, sipping white wine in a restaurant on a Greek island.

"With Adora you can stop time," reads the caption at the end of the video, while a dolly shot of smiling close-up faces, some moved to tears, parades by. Irene puts her earphones back in to respond to the assistant who appears on the screen: a blonde woman around her age, draped in an airy pink blouse.

"I'm Valentina, your treatment coordinator," the

woman says, putting a hand on her chest. "It's a pleasure to finally meet you in person, after our email exchange."

"My pleasure," Irene says.

"If it's all right with you, I'd like to start with an informative chat, then I'll ask you a few questions and go on to explain the course of treatment."

"Of course."

"Did you know that women of your age have a five percent monthly chance of pregnancy caused by unprotected sex? The chances of success are not very high and, in any case, it's actually not that easy to get pregnant. If you decide to proceed with the treatment, Adora will preserve your eggs using the vitrification technique. The method consists of ultra-rapid freezing: we submerge your eggs in liquid nitrogen at minus 196 degrees centigrade. Ultra-rapid freezing guarantees a higher survival rate of the oocytes, so that, until the time they are needed, the cells will remain unaltered. Once the freezing is complete, you will receive a photograph with the image of the oocytes that have been vitrified. So now: what made you think about freezing your eggs? Have you considered the option of surrogate motherhood? Have you planned the date of a possible pregnancy yet? Moving on to the financial investment ..."

The interview ends after forty-five minutes. When the screen returns to the fixed picture of the wallpaper, Irene observes her reflection in the monitor. Even more than her answers to the questions, the questions themselves irritated her. Because they were inevitable, or because they've been avoided until now. On the desk, her cell phone lights up: it's Valentina, the treatment coordinator. She's just sent her an email with the notes from their interview, her copy of the contract and the informed consent that she is to send back if and when, but in any case, as soon as possible. There's not much time left, that's clear: the thought of a countdown to the appointment makes her smile and then immediately stop.

In anti-fog mode, the motorcycle's headlights and the visor of her helmet turn red, tinging Milan with crimson, making the shapes of the visible houses clear and liquid, as though in a pool of water. Irene takes the longest but most enjoyable route to Via Saterna. She accelerates along a curve and imagines herself pregnant. She tries to picture the weight seen on the bodies of her sister and her friends. When she reaches her destination, she feels as if it's been months since the interview.

Upon arrival, she opens the gate and parks along the driveway, then retraces her steps to the mailbox; she finds the key where Ferrari had promised her it would be. The idea of actually starting to work, of doing something and planning the next steps, puts her in a good mood. She doesn't think about the girl until she enters the door and finds her there, sitting on the sofa waiting for her. She takes off her helmet, thinking about the conversation with Ferrari, and knows what she has to do, even if she won't do it today.

Within minutes, they are already down in the cellar. The walls are paneled in wood and there are low windows that open at the ceiling, overlooking the garden. The light is dim, and from a certain point on, it's impossible to venture any farther: crates of paintings and pieces of furniture block the way. At the far end, in the dark, Irene has the impression that she can make out the shapes of bulkier furnishings.

To begin with, they focus on a dozen or so cartons full of glassware, stacked at the entrance. Water glasses, cocktail glasses, wine glasses. The girl keeps her head down as she works, her hair tied back in a ponytail. At Irene's request, she has put on a pair of worn leather ankle boots with a crescent-shaped hole under the heel.

"Seventeen," she says, after running her finger along the base of each glass. "One is missing," or, "Twelve. Flower-shaped. Like a rose," or, "Look, these are cut crystal."

"They're scotch glasses."

"Eight scotch glasses, then."

"Write it on the right-hand side," Irene says, and she obeys, quickly jotting down the words with the marker.

The girl smiles at her often, and seems eager to make sure she satisfies her requests, if possible anticipating them. Every little courtesy she performs seems to move her farther away from the risk of being thrown out.

"Will these things be sold with the house?" the girl asks, opening yet another carton.

"That's right."

"So whoever buys the house will be buying everything, the glassware, the furniture, all of it. Is that how it's done?"

"Usually, yes."

"Are there times when that doesn't happen?"

"There could be a situation when the buyer doesn't like the furnishings, of course."

"And if that happens?" the girl says, holding a teaspoon with a crystal handle.

"Pretty," Irene says. "Do you want to keep it?"

The girl abruptly puts the teaspoon back in the carton as if it were scalding. "I would never do such a thing, I was just curious."

"I know, don't worry," Irene lies. "Everything here belongs to the creditors. If the buyer chose not to keep this stuff, the furniture and the accessories, down to the last spoon or fork, would be sold elsewhere."

"Understood."

"What did you say your name was?" Irene asks, pretending not to remember.

"Lidia."

"Sorry, I was in a rush yesterday," she says, handing her the notepad. "Let's switch jobs a bit, I'll count and you record. I always do the inventory at the beginning," Irene explains. "Then again at the end, before the viewings. When the cleaning and maintenance people come, I'll lock the cellar door, just as a precaution. There are twelve teaspoons. Write down: twelve coffee spoons with crystal handles."

"How long have you been doing this work?" asks Lidia.

"Sixteen years," Irene replies, then checks the side of the carton with the marker, and indicates the pile of boxes closest to the cellar door. "Push this one over there with the others."

They go on counting, recording, shifting cartons, but the girl doesn't let her work in peace. She keeps asking questions, a barrage of questions that in any other situation Irene would find nerve-racking, but that today, after the interview a few hours earlier, she finds unobjectionable, almost a kind of distraction.

"Are you a real estate agent?"

"No."

"But you sell houses."

"Only at auction."

"Do you like your job?"

"Very much."

"So how does it work?"

"An individual loses a lot of money or needs a lot of money or dies without heirs. I inspect the properties, compile my inventories, make the necessary improvements prior to the sale, advertise the property on the market, arrange for the auction, and close the deal."

"How many houses have you sold?"

"I don't keep track."

"More than a hundred? Less?"

Eighty-seven, Irene would like to tell her, since she always records her sales in an actual notebook, with paper pages. "Less," she says.

"What's the most beautiful house you've sold?"

"I couldn't say," she replies shortly.

The girl stops talking. From then on, they work in silence, surrounded by the tinkling sound of glasses and silverware being counted and shifted. They press on, taking turns and exchanging roles. There's no need to speak, Lidia is quick to catch Irene's nod and hold out her hands to receive or hand on an item. The girl is stronger than she looks: she handles the weight of the boxes with ease, she doesn't complain, she doesn't slow down. After a while, both of them sink into the trance of moving automatically, and Irene feels the pleasure of having emptied her mind with this unknown girl who obeys, makes little noise, oddly keeps her company.

After midday, the sun begins its descent, and what little light there is grows dimmer as well. Irene signals Lidia to stop. They stack the boxes against the wall, and it appears they have completed the supply of silverware and crystal. Lower, larger boxes await them, but lighting is required.

"You can take a rest," Irene tells the girl, before leaving the cellar. After passing the kitchen and returning to the living room, where it is still daylight, she sends an email to Ferrari to remind him of the need to restore the electricity. The notification of his response arrives as Irene reaches the door leading to the veranda: "Right away," Ferrari writes. The French door is locked. Irene tries to assess things from inside, then retrieves the keys and searches through the bunch for the right one. On the fourth or fifth attempt the door opens.

The girl has followed her, keeping a safe distance. Irene pretends not to have noticed her and steps outside. The construction of the veranda is astute. Four concrete columns, in good condition, support the high ceiling. The outer framework of the porches extends up to the attic, creating the deception of a square plan, in an area where plants and trees extended. Remaining from the previous period are clay archways on the gray marble, large emptied or broken flower pots, scratches of the roots on the glass. The path leads to the back entrance: the kitchen's French window faces the archway to the garden. The veranda door is unlocked, and the lock does not appear to have been forced.

Irene turns toward the girl, who continues walking behind her and who at that point gives her a guilty smile.

"I found it like that," she says. "The key was under that pot."

Irene simply shakes her head, but regrets her reaction, worried that the girl might interpret her tolerance as approval. She lengthens her stride, reestablishing the distance between them and assessing the garden. The trees have survived: two dark-leaved magnolias that stand at opposite corners of the boundary wall, while the rest is an unkempt lawn, a field of tall, listless weeds.

Irene continues along the edge of the veranda, stopping where the grass is not as tall, less overgrown. She sits on the ground, leaning back against the metal frame. The girl hesitates, then does the same. They sit in silence, gazing at the garden wall: a ten-foot-high barrier covered in ivy that shuts out the world. The creeper trails upward in all directions, luxuriant, its dense tentacles overrunning the ground, reaching toward the house.

Irene sketches and takes notes on her cell phone, too tired to go back for her notepad. She can sense the girl's persistent eyes on her.

"Everything okay?" Irene asks her.

"Sure," the girl replies; she's removed her shoes again, stretched her legs out in front of her; she returns Irene's look and folds her arms in her lap.

"Don't you have anything better to do?" Irene asks, making an effort to sound playful.

"Am I bothering you?" Lidia smiles at her for the first time, as if she were truly at peace, and Irene shrugs.

"You follow me everywhere," Irene says. "It doesn't change anything for me."

"I like the company. I'm always by myself. That's all."

"Okay."

"Your work seems interesting," the girl adds.

"And you?" Irene asks, looking away. "You said you study. What do you study?"

"Environmental biology. I study the biology of organisms. I want to specialize in biomonitoring."

"So is it true that in about fifty years we'll be extinct?" Irene jokes.

"It could happen sooner."

"Good to know. In any case, I'll be dead by then. I feel sorry for you."

The girl seems bothered by her cheerful banter; she lowers her eyes and sinks her feet into the grass. Irene looks at the sky: in the fog you can make out the sun's white disc, very small and distant, a detail that distinguishes good days from bad. If she were to give birth to a child now, even assuming she would spend the next forty years in perfect health, she would still have to leave him to face another forty years of living on his own. The morning's interview comes back again; her forehead is burning, even though it's starting to get chilly.

"The most beautiful house I've sold ..." Irene says, changing the subject. "Two or three years ago, I sold the home of a fashion designer. She had become ill, then isolated, and had stopped working on her collections. The villa was in Val di Rhêmes. When I arrived for the first inspection, all I found were garments; the house was empty. In recent times, she had been sleeping on the floor and eating canned tuna, but there were dresses everywhere. She died alone. I have never seen such designs."

Afterward, both remain silent.

In the courtyard, the child opens his arms, then brings his hands together in front of him: he remains still, fingers poised at his belly, as if he were holding a ball. Irene watches him from the window. It is starting to get dark, but he maintains his composed position, and his firmness has a commanding force. He is nine years old.

She hears her sister coming, announced by the rhythmic, decisive swish of the silk robe she is wearing. She comes up beside Irene and she too looks down from the window.

"Tai Chi," she says.

"I see." Irene studies her sister's profile. "Isn't he a little young for that type of thing?"

"It's mandatory," her sister replies, tying the belt around her waist. "They teach it at school now, it's wellbeing homework." When the headlights of a car fill the courtyard, projecting the boy's shadow onto the wall, Elena announces that the aesthetician has arrived. She goes to the sofa and gathers the cups from which they've been drinking matcha tea.

Irene watches her move. She is wearing soft eco-leather slippers that muffle the sound of her footsteps. When she gets to the entrance hall, she stops at a vase of lilies and straightens the stems. Irene sees her thinking, captured in the mirror on top of the chest. Elena sees her in the mirror and smiles brightly.

"Your time is precious, you can't spend it with someone who has prostate problems," Elena tells her point blank.

Irene has caught her in top form, fresh from a fifteen-day spiritual retreat in the Azores, two weeks of silence and intermittent fasting. When Elena opens the door to the aesthetician, inviting her into the house with a sweep of her arm, her back muscles strain the fabric, revealing the sculpted shape of her shoulder. Following her and the aesthetician upstairs, Irene notices the suggestions of the femorals along her thighs, two wooden carvings on her legs. Always, and in everything, her sister is solid, she too heir to the paternal body.

When they reach the guest room, Irene is introduced. She remains silent while Elena talks to the aesthetician, who then sets a large rigid beauty case on the floor, opens it, spreads a cloth on the dresser, and begins lining up glass vials one beside the other.

"Would you like to join in?" her sister asks, sitting on the bed.

"No."

"My treat," Elena insists solicitously. "When did you last have one?"

"I don't know, a year ago."

"But that won't do any good," Elena grumbles. "Come on, I won't take no for an answer. Can we both do it, Jini?"

"Of course," the aesthetician confirms, doubling the number of vials. Irene's sister waves her over to come sit next to her, and she obeys.

"A year ... You're not getting any younger, you know. Beauty is a matter of maintenance, right, Jini?"

The aesthetician, who is twenty-five at most and has a flawless amber complexion, nods seriously while tugging on a pair of latex gloves.

Irene observes her. Her thin, toned arms remind her of Lidia's, the skin on her neck is taut, adhering tightly to the body that hosts it. She seems to recognize the distinctive features of youth, elements that she overlooked until the day she realized that she no longer possessed them. Her sister also studies the girl, and Irene is sure that she is thinking the same things, though more harshly.

The aesthetician begins with the forehead, tracing the sites like compass points. During the injections, Elena remains expressionless. When it is her turn, Irene forces herself to stay still, despite the fact that the liquid stings. The girl is fast and precise. When the injections to her forehead are done, her sister pushes some plumped-up pillows toward the center of the bed, then slips off her panties. Irene looks at her questioningly.

"Haven't you ever done it there?", Elena asks.

"No."

"Take off your panties," she orders. "It works miracles."

She lies on her back, her torso supported by the pillows, her robe open on her belly, and pulls up her legs, hugging them to her chest with her arms. The aesthetician prepares another vial and Irene can't keep from grimacing. Elena smiles.

"Believe me, your life will change once you become aware of the amount of skin that sags from your body when you're over thirty."

"Idiot."

“No, it’s a general consideration. And anyway, it doesn’t do any harm. Relax.”

Irene shakes her head, fumbling with the zipper of her pants. She takes them off along with her panties and folds the items carefully. She watches herself lie back against the pillows and imitate her sister, unsure why she’s going along with it. For a moment, the image of her sagging sex had terrified her, a grotesque omen that she had never even contemplated before sitting down on the bed.

Turning to her, the aesthetician seraphically sprays disinfectant between her legs, wipes it with a cloth, and changes the syringe. The injections are painful. Elena is now laughing at the expression of regret that Irene can’t suppress. “Amateur.”

When the girl has finished, Irene starts to stand up, but her sister grabs her arm.

“Where are you going?”

“I’m getting up.”

“We have to stay like this for half an hour, otherwise the liquid will travel everywhere.”

“You’re kidding, right?”

“Dear, thank you very much,” Elena says to the aesthetician. “Just close the door of the room behind you when you leave. Everything is already paid for.”

The girl nods, seals the used syringes and cloths in a plastic bag, and quickly arranges the vials back in her beauty case. She says goodbye politely and goes out, leaving them both motionless, stretched out like turtles that have fallen on their backs.

“Did you pay for me too?” asks Irene, breaking the silence.

"Of course, an hour ago, before you said yes," her sister sighs contentedly.

"Thank you."

"Don't mention it."

"So, aside from all this, how are you?" asks Irene.

"Great. I've been seeing someone much younger than me, for a few months now. A new life."

"But what do you have to say to each other?"

"Nothing! At my age, at *our* age, there's no time for conversation anymore, and if you decide to ditch that old guy and try having sex with someone half your age, for once, you'd realize it too, and we wouldn't have to keep having these conversations."

Elena's wedding band gleams as she kneads her fingers into her thigh.

"There is no topic that can hold up in the face of the disparity, the gap that separates us from those born after us, there is no meaningful conversation to be had before the body of someone who has not yet begun to age: every other term of comparison is inadequate. The chasm between us and them," her sister says, "is infinitesimal and at the same time inescapable: we were them just moments ago, remember?"

"Apart from that, how are things going with Giovanni?" Irene asks.

"Okay," says Elena. "Raising three children is a feat, especially with Giovanni always away for work: lately he's been very stressed by the market's mad rush for water resources. Fortunately, the youngest is not as problematic as the twins, a real pair of teenagers at this point. Nowadays they seem to grow up less anxious. The things that would have worried us, that *did* worry us—all of us except you, Irene—don't seem to affect him. Maybe it's all that school time devoted to meditation, or maybe it's just that he takes after you. What do you think, Irene? Maybe it's a gift younger children have."

Irene smiles, listens to the chronicle of Elena's life: just as when they were kids, Elena has the same unsparing, feral vision. She still seems like an animal masquerading as a woman, her toned body sewn over her. Each time they meet, Irene is convinced that that's the very reason she loves her: it's a quality that has always made her prefer her to her older brother, so similar to their mother.

After thirty minutes, they get dressed. "Think hard about what I said," her sister says, walking her to the door. "Half your age."

Irene smiles, and before leaving squeezes her sister's forearm. Elena accepts the unexpected gesture of affection without comment.

"What's the house like?" she asks, when Irene is already halfway down the first flight of stairs.

"Fabulous," Irene replies.

Outside the door, she walks past the iron grillwork that encloses the courtyard. She waves to her nephew, caught up in the flow of a position. He looks at her unresponsively, and goes on watching her until she puts on her helmet and drives away on her motorbike. His childish face is a void in the rearview mirror.

1985

Saverio says that conferences are now a trend, and that conference tourism, because that's what it is, is one of the most perverse distortions of the decade. You always find yourself at the Savoy or the Exposition, with representatives from some Scandinavian country, in rare cases with delegates from Japan, the tribal recognition of lanyards and badges hanging around your neck; you attend sessions and walk a lot, you also talk a lot, you waste time in at least three different ways, all on the same day.

Saverio hates conferences, even when it's an important event for his firm, like today. He can't contain himself; he complains on the metro, looking at the shoes of women sitting nearby or passing in front of him. He observes a long pause of silence only when a girl with a pair of dark teal pumps sits down next to him. Adjusting his coat and his thick mass of gray hair, he looks at her only from the ankles down.

Dario turns his head away, embarrassed. At home, Carla's symptoms have gradually worsened over the past three weeks, leading to a trip to the ER last Monday, followed by an urgent visit with the specialist. Carla doesn't process glucose well, or something like that, he didn't fully understand, or at least doesn't remember. He was distracted throughout the conversation: it was the day the kitchen marble was being put in at Via Saterna. He knows that, for a moment, the possibility of miscarriage had been candidly discussed, and for that moment he had felt a great sense of hope and relief, thinking that Carla too must by now be tired of being so ill or that it was really impossible for her body to hold up. Then she'd said that she wanted this baby at any cost, just like that, to the doctor, without even looking at him or checking to see if he agreed, or letting him participate in that decision, though it was a decision that concerned him as well, his life, his future, something he too would have liked to discuss. The specialist had started tearing out prescriptions and instructions and had scheduled a series of precautionary checkups over the next six months, and Carla had emerged from the visit revitalized, less green than when she had entered the room.

Having reached their stop, Saverio starts talking again, his badge clutched in the same hand that conveys his contempt for the people they pass in the tunnels. His presence annoys Dario, who would have preferred to go to the conference alone, or not to go at all. He has an embryonic speech in mind, but the idea of speaking about the project in public bothers him, not so much because of the tangible discomfort of the collective gaze or the pressure of the audience, as because of an instinctive sense of danger, the possibility of suddenly finding himself revealed in a passion that lately, day by day, seems to him more illicit, inappropriate, monstrous. He can't help comparing his morbid feeling for Via Saterna—and therefore for Lidia—to the legitimate feelings that others seem to have; even Saverio's fetish for women's shoes seems innocent and pales by comparison, a game played out of boredom.

As they walk along in the chilly February sun, in sync with the crowds of participants headed to the Savoy, Dario is still thinking about the speech. Saverio, remote and somber, reminds him that today's events are sponsored by the Lombardy Region, and that any possible recognition—he repeats, *possible*, despite the fact that no competition is expected and the assignment of the title has already been discussed—will come directly from an administrative representative.

Once they've entered, Dario feels flushed, excited, all of a sudden the speech he has chosen turns out to be brilliant, elevating him above the reserved seats, the white chairs and the podium where the speakers alternate, the themes—*Building Contemporary Living*, *Project Venezia and a New Principle of Minimum Housing*—the clothes crumpled by the torture of the slides being projected. This feeling of egocentric levitation suddenly gives him a deep sense of well-being, and he finally sees his goal as being achieved.

When his speech is introduced, Dario takes his place on the podium, holding the organized notes he put together the night before: prominent at the top is the name that is also the project's title, *Via Saterna*.

The project was conceived by adopting the postmodernist principle of the circularity of events, he says, an idea of time that subverts the linear conception of past and future as moments that are successively erased, and that surpasses the temporality of the finalistic principle. The plan's canonical external square footprint is contradicted by the internal circular design, in which different elements of the space converge simultaneously. The house therefore exists in the relationships *between* components rather than in the components themselves, and is proposed as an organism that compels interpretation. The formulation of the interpretation modifies the import of the overall picture, alters its meanings, which are no longer stable but always hypothetical. The house is the reflection not only of its inhabitants, but of its guests. The design draws on an immense store of historical materials, art, cinema, fashion, advertising. The house becomes a panopticon, but also a temple, a place of pleasure, of spiritual retreat. The house performs, the atmosphere is festive and combinatorial.

Parallel to the official discourse, a secret one is taking place, the truth that links the plan to Lidia's financial support and her ill-advised willingness, to the absolute trust that she has placed in him, out of curiosity or rebellion. At the end of the speech, Dario discusses the publication of the project with enthusiastic representatives of the trade magazines, and mentions the assignment awarded by the regional official. The photos of Via Saterna will be featured in the monthly editions, and additional funding will follow.

"You did very well," Saverio says.

He's been by his side the whole time, following him closely during the interviews and introductions, determined to represent the studio and to remind everyone that Dario is, if not his direct property, at least his creation. Now he's swirling a spoon in his coffee, as they sit at a table in the hotel bar, among the survivors of the conference, including some official Japanese delegates. He even offered him a drink, something that has never happened since Dario started working for him, a far cry from the threats of dismissal that he was given only a year ago.

"I owe you my apologies," Saverio adds, his eyes continuing to shift, pausing on him, darting behind him, then all around. "I lacked the necessary vision to believe in this project."

Dario wonders if Saverio has ever possessed such vision: his studio survives on the inheritance from his father, a prominent name that has faded but that still ensures that he can live beyond the means of the young architects who work for him. Dario, who is no longer young, and who feels neither pity nor sorrow for him, particularly at this moment, wishes only to get away.

"As I was saying, I apologize," Saverio concludes. "Not now, but I would like to talk with you about some new possibilities for your figure. I would like to discuss your position and your salary again. I realize that you want to work with greater autonomy, and I am prepared to offer you that, while guaranteeing you the studio's protection. Continuing on alone would be too risky, Dario, that's what I would like you to understand. And at any other studio, regardless of any promises, you would be starting from scratch."

Dario lets him talk, focusing on the elegant reliefs of the porcelain china, which suddenly seem showy to him, as if that conversation had defiled them.

"Gladly," he replies, "we can talk whenever you want."

Saverio nods, and when Dario feels his euphoria about to deflate, he breaks away using Carla as an excuse: "She's not feeling so well lately, you know." Saverio lets him go, unable to conceal a frown of annoyance; for a moment he relishes the idea of not giving Dario what he wants or what he believes is already his—he'd like him to be excited at the announcement of a promotion, at the promise of a higher salary, he wants him to be grateful and appreciative, and forget that he predicted he would fail.

Leaving the hotel, Dario begins to walk, aimlessly at first, before finding himself nearing Via Saterna. He is aware of it from a distance, when it is not yet visible; it is not he who approaches the house, but the house that comes to him.

When he gets there, it's dark outside, and the lights in the house are on; loud music vibrates on the walkway and in his hand as he puts the spare key into the front door. Inside, the living room is brightly lit, but Lidia is not there. Before going up the stairs, Dario can't resist inspecting the kitchen, to check the installation of the marble. Certain of not being seen, he quickly crouches on the floor, to examine the grout.

Standing up again, he notices the presence of a bottle of red wine abandoned on the living room coffee table, as the music's volume increases further. He climbs the circular staircase heading for the second floor, which Lidia has selected as her refuge. Still used to being an only child, she has chosen the guest room in Pantone Green C for herself. Dario walks down the carpeted corridor to the room. From the doorway, he sees Lidia: she is wearing a tank top and a pair of white panties. Looking at herself in the wardrobe mirror, she musses her hair and makes an emphatic sensual move in front of her reflection.

When Lidia turns around, wearing makeup and flushed from the wine, Dario sees her dissolve into the background. As if by a surreal phenomenon, Lidia melts into the walls, begins to flow in the veins of the house, that's how he imagines her, while her arms reach out begging him to come closer: he dreams of her in the conclusive rite of creation—even if she is burning, even if he will have to tell her that it's all over. Not today—but it's over.

At dawn on Thursday, Irene receives a message from Ferrari notifying her that the utilities have been turned on in Via Saterna. She responds to an email from Adora's treatment coordinator, and a series of quick exchanges follow. A contract is signed, two medical prescriptions are sent, then an electronic order for the medicines is sent to the pharmacy along with a request for home delivery.

In the afternoon, Irene returns to Via Saterna to continue the inventory of the cellar. Lidia helps her catalog the linen and, during the breaks between one list and another, she keeps turning the lights in the rooms on and off, excited about having electricity. At the end of the day, when it's dark, Irene pauses a few minutes to look at the house from her motorbike—on the third floor, in the attic, a light turns on and off intermittently.

On Friday morning, Irene opens the package delivered by the pharmacy and begins taking the hormones. She receives a voicemail from Paolo, but doesn't listen to it. At Via Saterna, Lidia has some sort of asthmatic attack triggered by the dust. After having her drink some water and airing out the kitchen, Irene orders her not to set foot in the cellar. The girl stands in the doorway, watching her.

"Don't you have to study?"

"I have plenty of time to study."

At the end of the day, Irene can see that Lidia doesn't want to be alone over the weekend, so much so that the girl tries to detain her with questions about her work, asks her to tell about another house.

On Saturday, Irene has sex with a stranger on webcam and books a massage at a wellness center. In an email, Ferrari informs her of the imminent delivery of the floor plan. On Sunday, after dinner, her father falls asleep on the sofa and, as she goes past the living room door unnoticed, Irene sees her mother move the walker. With her foot, her mother nudges the metal frame a little further over, far enough away so that her father can only reach it by asking for help. Irene goes back upstairs without making a sound, and shortly afterwards she hears her mother leaving for mass.

Very early Monday morning, closing the door behind her at Via Saterna, Irene looks around for Lidia, who, unlike the previous days, is not there waiting for her. She searches the living room, then the kitchen, pushes against the cellar door, which is still locked as she left it on Friday, and walks through the garden. The girl's absence troubles her. Back inside, she goes up the stairs, and only halfway up the flight, when she is about to start searching the first floor, does she hear a noise: the rush of running water, a low but unmistakable sound. The acoustic trail comes from a source above, and Irene follows it up to the second floor, to the green room.

On the plastic sheet covering the bed are some objects and items of clothing. Water is running in the bathroom and the door is open. Smaller than the one in the master bedroom, the bathroom is notable for the position of the shower, planted in the center like a vertical wind tunnel. On the floor, a mosaic of pink and white tiles extends in all directions and up the walls, as far as the ceiling. Light comes from the east-facing veranda and from the slim metal lamps that hang from the ceiling, all lit, as if the shower ritual had been going on since the dark hours of the night.

Irene can't avoid seeing Lidia, who is facing away from her, naked under the stream of water, scrubbing her neck and arms, persistently removing the dead skin. The glass gives her body the iridescence of marble. Irene watches her bend down to soap her hands, revealing her rosy sex, then straighten up, rubbing a palm between her legs: the foam runs off in a trickle between her round buttocks.

Irene looks away from Lidia's body, and goes to the bed. On the mattress she finds some underwear, a book, and a small leather shoulder bag. She glances at the volume, *Memories of an Entomologist*, then, alert to any change in the sound coming from the shower, she opens the bag. In the first compartment is a shiny silver object, which Irene takes out to examine: a lighter engraved with Solomon's knot. The second compartment holds an ad with a QR code printed on it and an old paper ID card. Irene frames the code with her cell phone and starts loading the page, then takes out the ID card. A faded close-up of Lidia is affixed to a scant description of her physical features and her place of birth, Milan. Irene quickly looks at the date of birth, her surname—Castelli—then refolds the document. She is about to put it back in the bag, when she has a funny feeling. She unfolds it again, skims through the information, and stops again at the date of birth: February 23, 1966. She reads it again, before putting the ID card back where it was.

She places the shoulder bag back on the bed and

returns to the door. Lidia is still in the shower, her arms clasped around her chest and her face turned up to the jet of water.

Irene goes downstairs with a knot in her stomach: Lidia is walking around with a fake ID card and she can't think of any honest reason why anyone would possess a false document. Back at the cellar door, she unlocks it. She doesn't know how to handle her discovery, since she found the ID while snooping through this stranger's private things. She regrets not having gotten rid of Lidia immediately, as Ferrari had suggested. Troubled, she starts pacing through the room, thinking about the order in which to tackle the work.

"You're here early."

Irene turns around, startled. Lidia's voice behind her in the dark cellar made her jump.

"You have to stop scaring me!"

Lidia makes a childish pout. She remains outside the door, in the circle of light from the window. Drops of water trail from the tips of her wet hair down to the floor, pooling at her feet. She's wearing a white tank top and panties, and she's holding a large rock. Irene stares at it for a few seconds. She feels a shiver that quickly turns to fury.

"I was taking a shower. I heard noises..."

Irene doesn't give her time to finish her sentence: she takes two steps and grabs her wrist. The girl puts up no resistance as Irene snatches the stone from her hand, opens the French door and throws it into the garden, hitting the ivy-covered wall.

"I'm sorry," Lidia murmurs. "I was scared too. It's seven in the morning. You always come late ..."

"Who else could it have been?"

"How do I know. Milan is dangerous, I'm here alone."

Irene shakes her head. She steps away from the girl, and goes to the light switch in the cellar. For a moment she regrets her reaction, and feeling ashamed only makes her even more furious.

"I'm sorry … I'll go get dressed and come down to help you," Lidia says contritely.

"No, I'll do it myself," Irene replies, tackling the crate containing a large dining table a second later.

The morning proceeds with the uncrating of the furniture: Irene cuts the plastic and cardboard packaging with a pair of large scissors, uncovering wood, glass. The furniture appears to be in excellent condition; apart from the dust it looks like new. Lidia gets dressed and comes back almost immediately, sitting on the step at the doorway to the cellar, she watches her in silence, goes away for a few minutes, comes back with a book, reads. Irene pretends she's alone, and the girl accepts her silence, making no attempt at conversation.

Around one o'clock, when it's time to go, Irene finds Lidia sleeping. She's curled up between the wall and the door, her head resting on her knees, like a pet dog. Looking at her, for a moment Irene considers waking her up, then changes her mind and leaves her there asleep. She goes back to the living room, puts on her jacket and retrieves her backpack; rummaging around, she scoops out the motorcycle keys with two fingers, and instinctively feels around for her card holder. Not finding what she's looking for, she turns the backpack upside down, and dumps her gloves, earphone case, and balaclava on the sofa. The credit cards are gone, yet she's sure she's put them in her bag, as she does whenever she goes out—a meticulous habit. She immediately thinks about the backpack left unattended all morning, and right after that of Lidia, who has been going in and out undisturbed, and about the fake document.

Irene retraces her steps to the kitchen, where Lidia is still sleeping. Bending over her, she reaches out, and shakes her by the shoulder. The girl wakes up with a start, frightened.

"Where are the credit cards?"

"What?"

"I said where are my credit cards?"

"What credit cards?" Lidia asks, standing up, bewildered.

Irene realizes that what's infuriating her is not just the idea that the girl tried to rob her, but her defenseless, unshakably innocent look. Enraged, she cries, "I left my credit cards in my backpack this morning, and now they're gone. Did you take them?"

The girl widens her eyes, distraught. "I don't know what you're talking about."

"You took them."

"I would never do anything like that, I'm not a thief."

"Give them back to me."

"I'm not a thief, I didn't take anything!"

Irene takes two steps back, looks at Lidia, who is pale now, even paler than she usually is. "You're a liar," she tells her. "You go around with false documents, you're a thief."

The girl's face gives way to surprise, then fear. "You searched through my things?"

“What was I supposed to do? I let you stay, I believed you. I had to make sure ...”

“I gave you my word.”

“I don’t even know who you are.”

Lidia lowers her eyes, shakes her head. She tightens her arms around her body. “I can’t use it to steal. I found it here and I kept it.”

“Bullshit! It’s your photo!”

The girl simply gives her a sidelong glance, starts to put a finger in her mouth, but stops midway. She rubs an arm and looks at her sadly again, without speaking.

“It’s not what you think, I can’t do anything with it.”

“Get out.”

Lidia doesn’t answer.

“I don’t want to find you here when I come back.”

Irene leaves the girl huddled against the wall, goes to the living room, and retrieves her backpack. She considers the thought of having achieved a victory, yet she feels shaken, fraught with anxiety. She slams the front door behind her furiously, shocked by the severity of her own turmoil. She feels lightheaded, her hands are sweaty, and there’s a lump in her throat. Thoughts of her parents’ actions at home, her father’s words, her sister’s steady gaze, the children gravitate around her, all at the same time.

Reaching the motorbike, she puts her hands in her jacket pockets to look for her keys, and along with the keys finds the leather case in which she keeps her credit cards. For a few seconds, she doesn’t move; she can’t forgive herself for not having checked there too, the most obvious place, before accusing Lidia. She looks at the entrance to Via Saterna, afraid that the girl has opened the door, as on the first day, and is watching her: the door is closed, the way she left it.

She puts the card holder back in her pocket, zips up her jacket, and pulls on her helmet. She climbs onto the motorbike, starts the engine, and for a moment Lidia is a distant problem. But then she can't bring herself to drive away. She's made an unjust accusation. She feels the sweat spreading from her hands to her neck and has to turn off the engine, take off her helmet to breathe.

Before she's decided to, she is walking back down the pathway. She fiddles with the keys, snaps open the lock, and steps inside, but suddenly something catches her arm, forcefully. Irene crashes to the ground. As she falls, she feels something cut into her skin, then the pain. On her knees, she stares at her hand, the sleeve still caught on the door handle. The jacket is ripped up to the forearm, and the sharp tip of the spring latch has carved a vertical groove on her skin.

Irene extricates the sleeve, and closes a hand over the wound. She gets back on her feet, still dazed, and finds herself facing Lidia, standing in the doorway. She hopes the girl didn't see her flop to the ground like an idiot.

"Listen," Irene says, out of breath, kicking the door shut behind her. "You have to forgive me, I was wrong."

The girl looks at her warily. Her face is blotched from crying. Irene recalls the words she spoke to her, the contempt with which she told her to get out.

"I had the cards. I usually never put them in ..." she says, spreading her arms. "I'm sorry." She goes over to Lidia, walking around the sofa. "I apologize."

Lidia sniffs. Then she nods, shrugging. "It' okay," she says, pointing. "You're bleeding."

Irene looks down. The first drops of blood have spattered the floor. "I don't even know how I did it."

"Come on, I'll help you," the girl says.

Irene follows her. Blood doesn't generally bother her, but she notices with alarm that she feels kind of dizzy. Once in the kitchen, she sits at the built-in countertop, as Lidia suggests. She watches her go to one of the boxes they've already inventoried, one full of kitchen linens, and take out a white napkin.

"No, not that one, that one is trimmed with Burano lace," Irene entreats.

Lidia rolls her eyes and puts the napkin back in the box.

"There are dish rags in the one next to it."

The girl uncovers the box full of dishcloths. Irene watches her carefully select one before returning to her; she unfolds the cloth, grabs the two ends, and rips it in half with a firm yank. Then she folds one of the edges and turns on the faucet in the sink. They both watch the rusty-colored water run, before it turns clear. Lidia spreads the cloth under the stream of water and soaks it.

"Hold out your arm."

Irene displays the wound: the skin is torn but the lesion is superficial.

Lidia sniffs again. There are swollen, purple blotches on her cheeks. She avoids Irene's eyes. Irene watches as she takes the dry half of the cloth and wraps it around her arm.

"I'm sorry," she tells her.

Lidia doesn't answer. She gently turns Irene's hand

until the palm is facing upwards, then draws it closer and rests the back of it against her sternum, to make it easier to secure the bandage.

"It must be the treatment I started," Irene continues, in a low voice. In the silence of the house, it is impossible to perceive Lidia's breathing: it is as if she were there but non-existent. Irene can feel the warmth of her hand, but there is no other evidence to prove that both are actually there. The dizziness tapers off to an ache at her temples, and Irene wants to say that she doesn't feel well. "They're having me take a lot of hormones."

"What kind of treatment is it?" Lidia asks.

"A fertility treatment."

There is no pity or commiseration in the girl's eyes, just what seems to Irene like frank curiosity, tolerable because it's emotionless.

"I'm trying to have a child," she says. "Or at least I think so."

Lidia tucks the corners of the bandage under at Irene's wrist, then moves the arm away from her chest and places it by her side.

"For months I washed up at the station," Lidia says out of the blue, with no apparent logical connection. "Or else, I went to those areas where they set up camps for the homeless. You can stand in line in the cold for as long as two hours before being able to wash. Sometimes I managed to sneak into a public swimming pool, very late at night, and I'd take a shower there. I'd walk home with my face steaming."

Irene doesn't speak, unsure of what to say. Lidia shrugs.

"You want to have a baby?" she asks, stepping back to the wall.

Irene can't believe that the first conversation she's having on this topic is with a stranger half her age.

"Yes, I think so."

"What do you mean?"

"What do you mean, what do I mean?"

"Either you want it or you don't want it."

"It's not that simple."

"Maybe it isn't for people your age," Lidia replies. "For people my age, everything is clearer."

For a long minute, they remain silent. Outside, the remote sound of flapping wings can be heard, or maybe it's just an electric car going by on the street.

"Last year, I had an abortion," Lidia adds. "Keeping it was never an option, but every now and then I think that on some days I would feel less alone, maybe I would be less afraid."

Irene can't keep from staring at her. Lidia lets herself be scrutinized without putting up any resistance; she never looks away, absorbing Irene's gaze with the imperturbable air of an oriental divinity.

"I found the ID card here in the house, in a drawer, and I took it. I just glued my photo on it."

"Do you need it to get around?" Irene asks, confused. "To pass through the security checkpoints?"

"When was the last time you were in Milan?" Lidia asks.

"My parents live here. I was born and raised here."

"Me too," says Lidia. "But how long has it been since you walked around? I mean outside the area of these neighborhoods?"

"I don't know ..."

"Getting from one side of the city to the other is a real effort. The eastern border is filled with electronic checkpoints outside and inside the stores, at bus stops, in hospitals: without having a document scanned you can't get through. Nobody accepts old paper ID cards anymore, they only want digital cards. It was just an impulse, I can't do anything with that document."

Irene reconstructs the scraps of news she's read online, the growing social tensions, the increased pressure exerted on the big cities by internal migration, her mother's frightened comments, Ferrari's remark about the border walls. Modulating her ideas about the present always provokes profound uneasiness. Besides, talking about current events doesn't seem to do anyone she knows any good: the reality is inevitable and plain to all, aside from news and forecasts—or at least that's the belief among those in her circle. Irene feels a sense of weariness come over her, slowing down her stream of thoughts. Reflexively, she rubs her temples.

"I'm exhausted."

Lidia nods. "Me too."

"We'll stop here for today," Irene says; she doesn't know if she's talking about the disagreement, this specific conversation, or their confessions. "Thank you for helping me. I'll be back tomorrow."

Lidia doesn't answer, and Irene lowers her sleeve around her arm to cover the bandage. The girl follows her to the door, though she stops a distance away, near the sofa. Irene takes one last look to examine the handle; traces of her blood remain on the spring latch.

"You don't have to leave," she says to the girl, stepping out the door.

Lidia, seated on the sofa, gives her a grateful smile.

1985

On December 25, *It's a Wonderful Life* is broadcast on TV, a film that Dario has always found grim, but that Carla doesn't mind. She has been saying that since they got married, or since the arrival of their firstborn. Every Christmas, after putting the children to bed, Carla, remote control in hand, searches for *It's a Wonderful Life* and says she doesn't mind it; over time, he has stopped telling her that he finds it grim. Today, too, they are on the sofa, exhausted, after fifteen hours of overeating, plus all the excitement, the screaming, the arguments over the gifts. Carla, who only smokes on special occasions, lights a cigarette and tucks her legs under her bottom.

Dario is only marginally aware of Carla. In the little time he spends at home, she is always in the back of his mind, a white noise. Depressed by the film, he shifts his gaze a little, starts thinking about Via Saterna again, about the work that is almost finished. In the rare idle moments, all he does is walk around the perimeter of the villa, up and down the stairs, looking for a flaw, an imperfection in the design that becomes visible, as per the rules, when it is too late to fix it. Consequently, he also thinks about Lidia, the same way he thinks about the house, going from one to the other.

"Dario." Carla jabs him in the side with the edge of the remote control. "Dario? Are you there?"

"Yes, sorry."

"Hmph!" Untangling her cramped legs, she stretches them out in front of her, and looks at her thin, stocking-covered calves. "There's something ..."

Carla looks at him with her round, blue eyes. She really seems to know, is inevitably about to speak. Instead, she looks at her ankles again and exhales cigarette smoke toward her toes, taut in their nylon membrane.

"I'm pregnant."

Her voice is drowned out as the soundtrack on the TV surges. Dario grabs the remote control from Carla's hand and turns off the TV.

"What did you say?" he asks her.

"I'm pregnant."

Carla looks at him, continues watching him as if waiting for his capitulation—she must know, or at least suspect. It can't be about Lidia, of course, about Via Saterna, but now he thinks there's something spiteful in her expression—*the party's over*, she seems to be telling him. *Where did you think you were going? You have two children, almost three, what did you think you were doing? That woman is just a girl.*

"That's great."

Carla smiles, exposing her incisors, and brings the cigarette to her lips again. She takes a long, greedy drag.

Dario reaches out and takes the cigarette from her fingers, stubbing it out on the bottom of his glass.

"And when ...?" he asks.

"I don't know, it's been about two months since the last time we fucked."

"Two months?"

"Right. Don't you remember? You were there too." Carla's victorious smirk turns into a tragic mask. "We probably did it three or four times in the last year."

"I don't think this is the time for recriminations," Dario snaps, disguising his angst.

He has no memory of that encounter, no matter where he burrows in his memory, all he finds is Lidia, her body, her intimate apparel, her voice. Then, faintly in the background, the trail of sex with Carla emerges, an evening when she must have decided to doom him, as she's doing now, an evening when he must have given in so as not to arouse her suspicions.

"You don't seem happy," she persists.

"What are you talking about? Of course I am. Just give me a moment to process it."

"There's nothing to process. I'm expecting a baby."

"I know, but it wasn't planned."

"Okay, it happened. So what? Aren't you happy about it?"

Dario stands up with the excuse of getting rid of the glass in which he snuffed out her cigarette. He walks the distance between the living room and the dining area, then back again, and when he returns, she's still there waiting for him. Now she's flopped in the armchair.

"It's not that I'm not, but it's not a good time for me," Dario says, standing in front of her. "With the project still going on, I won't be able to be there as much as I'd like."

"I can't stand hearing you talk about that project anymore."

The twinkling lights hanging from the tree rhythmically flash green and red across Carla's face.

"But I never talk about it," Dario replies, stuffing his hands in his pockets.

"It's as if you were constantly talking about it! You're always at the construction site, even when you're here at home you're at the construction site, in that other damned house, and you think about it incessantly." Carla's mouth quivers. "That's what I'm trying to say, I feel as though I can hear your thoughts, always on the project, on the construction site, as if you were talking about it all the time."

"You're being dramatic."

"I'm not being dramatic. You've been absent for a year, you forget things, you're in another world, you don't even see me."

For a moment he contemplates telling her the truth, letting it all out and confessing, something that will definitely never happen, not now, not at this moment, not ever. And yet, for an instant, he thinks of doing it, though he has never considered it before, busy as he's been pursuing the trail of the house and Lidia. Thinking back to the past year, which Carla reproaches him for as if he were at fault, he struggles to calculate, and gets lost in the math: everything seems to him to have just begun, or to be never-ending, he wishes a miracle would suddenly materialize and that Via Saterna would roll back to its origins, that he could start over from the day he set foot there and the design worm began to eat at him, to devour him ...

"Dario!"

Carla is crying. She's still there, she hasn't gone away.

"I'm happy," he says. "I'm just very tired." Dario sits down next to her, and she immediately wraps her arms around her belly. "You know how important it is that this project succeeds, you know that, not just for me: for our family. I have no choice."

That's really how it was, he'd like to tell her, at least at the beginning. His initial objective was really nothing more than being able to free himself from the condition of subservience to the job, to guarantee himself, by completing the project, a broader space in the world. To stop counting money, to not count it and then regret it. And Carla, he would like to tell her, you were the first to want more, to want to look like a winner.

Dario listens to himself talking; on a deeper level, he listens to himself thinking about what a man whose wife is a few months pregnant should think. Everything that his life should be has become a screen behind which his real existence seems to exist. Obsessive, chaotic, with Lidia in the middle, and with the house on Via Saterna, which he never wants to complete. If he could, he would tear down the neighboring properties, the entire block, he would continue working on his construction, finally free.

Carla turns her head. She looks exhausted.

"Is there someone else?"

"There's no one else," Dario replies evenly.

Just like that, the conversation begins and ends, she falls silent again, and in the days that follow she starts feeling sick and begins to lose weight. Or maybe she's been feeling sick and losing weight for at least two months, Dario isn't sure. Nonetheless, or maybe precisely because she feels confined by that malaise, Carla does not cancel the weekend at her parents' house in Liguria: on Thursday evening she leaves with the children. As agreed, he remains in the city to supervise the laying of the external paving at Via Saterna.

That Thursday night he leaves with Lidia, heading to Como to spend a weekend at the lake, at her mother's villa, planned some time ago. Lidia lets him drive her car and falls asleep in the passenger seat. Upon arrival, he tells her to wait for him inside while he unloads the few bags. When he joins her, the room is cold; from the window, the water seems like a dark maw yawning at the foot of the valley. Lidia stirs as soon as Dario approaches the bed, even though he's been careful not to make any noise or turn on the light. As if an alarm were connected to her body, she searches for him in the languor of sleep, strokes his thighs, pins his face between her legs: though his skin, through clothing and underwear, Dario hears her breathing, her mouth open, then closed around him.

"On the Lecco branch of the lake there is a short river: it flows for a few months a year from a cave, but no one has ever managed to find its source. Legend has it that a beautiful woman promised to marry the man who was able to trace its source, but whoever ventured into the cave later came out inexplicably aged, raving about a marvelous parallel world populated by nymphs. They call it Fiumelatte, the River of Milk."

In the morning, Lidia points to the window, tracing an imaginary path that could take them from their hideaway to their destination. Her hand attempts to draw a new map, but pauses confusedly in mid-air, suspended over the blanket.

"At some point you get to the Orrido in Nesso—my

father used to take me there every now and then. We would look down. I don't know if I could do it now; just the thought of looking out over that ravine makes me dizzy."

She raises her head and looks up at him, smiles, then looks outside again.

"Over there." She points her finger beyond the ridge of houses and trees rimming the shore. "Over there is the Villa Pliniana. You can only get there by following a path through the woods. In the 1800s, it was the refuge of two lovers. It is said that they never left the house and that, at midnight, during the summer, they would wrap themselves in a white sheet and jump together from the balcony into the lake. The end of the love story was bound to cause the death of one of them."

Dario closes his eyes and listens. From the first day, Lidia's voice, her modulation, has prompted a specific resonance. Listening to her speak is to always respond to a command, even now that she delights in taking them places they haven't yet been and where she doesn't suspect they'll ever be able to go. He tries to focus solely on her voice, stripping the words of meaning and listening to her as if it were the sound of water breaking on the rocks.

"In that direction, inland, there's La Casa Rossa. The villa is abandoned, it's haunted. When I came here on vacation as a girl, the people from the area enjoyed scaring me with stories of a woman's screams and a piano that played itself. They said that the count's wife had killed herself for love in the villa, and that her blood gushed from the fountain."

Dario instinctively reaches out a hand, searching

for her lips. When he finds them, he closes his fingers over them and again, with his eyes closed, he feels her laughing against his palm.

"Those stories give me the shivers, stop it," he orders, loosening his hold.

He feels her shrugging off the covers, straddling him. "Why are you in such a bad mood, can you tell me?" She breathes against his closed eyelids to annoy him, until he opens his eyes again. "You've been impossible all week, what's wrong?" She is gripped by a frenzy that Dario has seen before, when she's afraid of showing she's upset: she evades the risk by repeating a sequence of small actions. She adjusts an earring, looks down and to the left, as if someone beside her were lurking or waiting for her. More often she resorts to tiny erotic gestures, runs a finger over her lip, revealing a glimpse of her lower incisors, or grazes her sternum, sliding a fingertip into her cleavage. Sometimes, like now, she starts tormenting him by mussing his hair, scraping an imaginary stain off his chest. She seems to live in fear that something won't happen, and Dario clearly recognizes his sense of guilt. Something is indeed about to not happen, he doesn't know when, or how, but soon something won't happen.

"I'm thinking about the house," he says, to reassure her.

"Me too," she replies.

"You too?"

"Yes. I'm thinking about it too. It's completed."

"I'm worried," Dario adds.

"Why?"

"Because I can't correct anything anymore. If there's

a mistake, it already exists, and sooner or later it will come out."

"I'll be there to point it out to you, if that mistake even exists."

Lidia is no longer smiling and slowly pushes herself back, freeing herself from the tangle of sheets. Spread open on him, she rubs her naked sex on his thigh; bracing her palms on his shoulders, she slides down to his groin and lower, pressing against him. The idea of bringing up Carla's pregnancy suddenly becomes terrifying, as Lidia begins to moan, looking at him as if waiting for him to give her permission, while at the same time fiercely indifferent to any signal.

The weekend they have planned, the first on the eve of their mutual intentions of liberation—Lidia newly emerged from her broken engagement, he now close to leaving Carla—takes place in compliance with the protocols of secrecy.

Since they can't socialize, they drink a lot, and on Sunday morning, Lidia, inspired by the urge to cleanse, works out on the terrace.

Dario watches her. She's in a pink lycra leotard, naked and tanned, her black terrycloth socks rolled up at the ankles. Oblivious to the cold, she works out with her headphones clamped around her head, holding her Walkman in one hand. Dario stands at the window, wrapped in a blanket, chilled to the bone. In the distance, beyond her body with its small, rippling back muscles and rounded behind, lies the lunar solitude of the lake, its mist bluish over the water. Over her shoulders, the possible trajectories of all their imaginary selves take flight, venturing off together or apart.

The day after Irene's injury, and the day after that, and the day after that one, Lidia behaves as if a contract had been signed that binds her to Irene's reliance on her. The girl's tendency to make herself useful becomes submissive; her desire to please, to guarantee her innocence at the cost of an endless list of tasks, is increasingly evident. She carries boxes, moves furniture, persists in returning a series of amphorae found in the cellar to their place in the garden. Irene tries to put up a mild resistance, but Lidia, undaunted, responds by smiling and going on with what she's doing. Soon her dedication turns into a hypnotic routine; for Irene it becomes enjoyable to watch Lidia move around and tire herself out, to communicate this or that request, to see her eagerly carry out her assignments.

In the last few days Lidia has been talking a lot, continuing her interrogations about Irene's work assignments, and often also telling her about her studies. The house still needs cleaning, but the cellar is almost empty, the inventory completed.

One afternoon, only five or six large paintings, carefully sealed in black plastic sarcophagi, remain to be moved. Lidia walks around the corners of the frames, uncertain how to proceed. Irene watches her leave a fingerprint on the veil of dust that covers the plastic wrapping.

"Will you help me carry them over there?"

The girl nods, grabs the frames, lifts, shoves, and

walks backwards, letting Irene guide her. The last canvases are tall and heavy, they barely fit through the cellar door. When they're done, they're both out of breath. Irene goes to the sofa and swipes the screen of her cell phone. The night before, Ferrari finally sent her the file of the three-dimensional plan. Some of the data is corrupted, he wrote her: not everything will be legible. Irene had been about to view the projection on the ceiling of her room at home, but the thought of Lidia had stopped her. She thought the girl would like to see it, too; for a moment, she'd imagined sharing the first look as a reward. She'd immediately had second thoughts, feeling presumptuous and at fault.

The treatment has continued on course and Irene continues to adhere to the plan. Each day she is more conscientious in taking the medication and each day less sure of her motives. One of the stimulants, the one taken in the morning, is enclosed in a transparent capsule that contains a bright, pink liquid—Irene can feel her breasts swelling, becoming taut, her skin tightening and turning red. In mirrors, she is aware of her body's attempt to make itself hospitable. The mellowing doesn't stop at her physical features; it seems to extend to her thoughts as well. She often finds herself thinking about Lidia with undue tenderness, almost as if the girl were her responsibility, or at least a problem to be concerned about.

"I wanted to show you something," she tells her now.

Lidia is still standing rigidly next to the paintings. There's something ridiculous about her posture, she's frozen in place, as if Irene's voice has caught her in an intimate moment.

"Is everything okay?" Irene asks her.

Lidia nods, puts her hands on her hips and walks closer.

Irene reaches for her backpack, takes the portable projector out of the bottom and connects it to her phone. She enjoys Lidia's confused look as she goes to the center of the room and puts the projector on the floor, near the circular pool.

"I wanted to show you the house," Irene says, starting the projection.

The image spills out, blurred and imprecise, filling the space, flooding the available surfaces and crossing their bodies. Lidia lowers her head to watch a purple stain spread across her shirt, then looks at Irene, bewildered.

"Wait, just a sec," Irene says, scrolling the image on her phone.

The projection steadies, the pixels recompose on the walls, bringing along the outline of the furnishings, a dream that rewinds. Once the furniture is recomposed, it's easier to work on aligning the shapes. When Irene's finger shifts the projection, lining up the two versions of the sofa—the actual one and the reproduced image—Lidia's breath catches.

"See?"

Last comes the light: it falls on the projection of the silver basin, in a past when it was still full of water. The sun splashes the walls with a burst of liquid reflections, in a way that is quite realistic and dazzling.

Lidia looks around wide-eyed. The projection recomposes itself when her movement disrupts it, and where it fails to reach, the outline of their shadows remains to reveal the sham: the dirty floor of the present bears no comparison to the reproduction's polished one.

"Do you know how it works?" Irene asks.

"I've heard about it," Lidia replies, studying her surroundings. "My university was about to buy one, then the funding was withdrawn."

"I bought this one with the money from an assignment, two years ago. I was left with nothing, but it was worth it," Irene says. "You just need enough photographs, the software does the rest."

Lidia approaches the basin, and Irene follows her. They both look into the water: on the silvery bottom a smaller circle of white stone can be seen, and within the white stone is another stone, round and black.

"There was still sunlight," Lidia notes.

"Yes," says Irene, struck by the thought of Lidia's age: she is so young that she has no memory of the city without fog.

The girl raises an arm, interfering with the trajectory of the reflection on the far wall. She toys with the white patterns of water collected in her hand.

"It's fantastic."

Irene crosses the room toward the entrance. She records the position of the low glass table, and that of the more imposing one, the dining table, a little further on, parallel to the curve of the veranda. Projected through the glass, you can see the garden on a beautiful day, and it's easy to make out the ivy climbing along the perimeter wall. She takes note of the arrangement on her cell phone.

"When were the photos taken?" Lidia asks.

Irene expands the image of the detailed floor plan on the screen.

“1986,” she replies, then runs her finger over the first floor file: the projection around them changes. The reproduction of the bedrooms appears.

Irene reduces the size of the image and moves it to Lidia, surrounding her: now the girl towers over the circle of rooms, still in the empty center, with the projection of the house around her like a hula hoop. Lidia, her expression serious, observes the sequence of rooms on the first level, then the second, and finally the attic. Disappointed by her lack of reaction, Irene selects the projection of the terrace last and expands the image again. The living room fills with laurel and viburnum shrubs, the red silhouettes of maples in the four corners.

Lidia starts to explore the terrace, moving around the intangible confines of the skylight. The virtual sun rays give her hair the sheen of silicon.

“Beautiful,” she says. “You can turn it off now.”

Irene complies, and the house empties.

“Do you have to leave?” Lidia asks.

“Yes, soon.”

“Do you want to take a walk with me?” she says.

“Where to?”

“I’d like to show you another house,” the girl replies, with an enigmatic smile.

As they move along Via Dante, staying close to the walls of the buildings, Lidia asks Irene if she can try on her anti-fog glasses. She puts them on and walks a few feet, looking around excitedly. “They really work.” Then she gives them back to her. “Hide them under your shirt. Hook them onto your bra. It’s better not to walk around with expensive stuff in sight."

Irene follows her advice, and wonders if the idea of indulging Lidia and giving in to her curiosity isn't riskier than she imagines. She's immediately ashamed of her fear, a sensation that makes her feel old and slow. Beside her, the girl walks confidently through the fog.

"It's not so bad today," Lidia says. "You can see well enough right now. I like walking from here to the border."

She's always tried to stay on this side, Lidia explains, because everything is more difficult on the other side: finding a safe room, keeping it, keeping an eye on it. There are very few people to the west, a real wasteland: it seems no normal person can afford to live here, the girl says, shrugging. Irene listens to Lidia's version—some of the constructs are familiar to her: the redistribution of residents is a process that began many years ago, when she was still involved in the traditional real estate market. In one way or another she had been part of the relocation changes but she hadn't stayed long enough to assess its effects. During her brief returns for family visits or business trips, the desertion of West Milan had never settled in her consciousness. For Irene, staying in the house of her adolescence now, making the same trip to Via Saterna every day, has meant needing to reflect on the exodus.

"Only tourists come here," Lidia goes on. "They roam around the center with glasses like yours, they almost never venture to the other side, and yet there are so many things to see over there, if you know how to get around." Irene responds with a smile and the girl seems relieved by her sign of encouragement; she plays at being her guide in a world that, if the rule of age applied, Irene should know better than she does.

As they near the Duomo, the figures in the shadowy gloom multiply, specters moving quickly in all directions, their trajectories extending from the intersection of Piazza dei Mercanti and Via Mengoni.

"Have your document ready," Lidia says, before withdrawing into silence.

Irene unlocks her phone screen, and tries to think of the last time she visited the center: it's been many years, enough to make her feel like a stranger.

The barriers are only visible from close up. Similar to a fence, they close off the view of the Duomo and disappear into the fog, metal walls nine or ten feet high, guarded by the military: four trucks parked on either side, soldiers patrolling. Documents must be presented at the turnstiles: like at a subway station, the ID card or drivers license must be swiped over the electronic eye. In the last two years, Irene has seen similar checkpoints in Rome, Florence, maybe even Venice, but never up close. She's only heard of some of these inspection checks, but has never had to pass through one, except for toll booths on the autostrada.

At the crossing there is a modest line waiting, and the soldiers keep watch from a distance, their faces hidden by anti-fog helmets. Lidia goes through ahead of her, and Irene follows, wondering once again whether it wouldn't be more prudent to step back and refuse the invitation at the last possible opportunity. Before she can hesitate, the line presses close behind her and others queue up at the exit.

Once past the border, Lidia heads immediately

toward the tunnel, sheltered from the open space, where the flow of traffic converges. In the background, the dark mass of the Duomo stands out like the belly of a waiting mother ship, its features blurred, the facade dissolved.

As they proceed toward Corso Vittorio Emanuele, the spectral figures grow more numerous, the noise increases. Vague outlines of bodies swarm around them, discernable only from close by, crossing their path and overtaking them, many with their faces covered to protect themselves from the vapors. Inevitably, her recollection is superimposed on the scene, especially when Irene guesses their destination. The idea of the crowd moving unseen, so close to her, disturbs her, so she quickens her pace and stays close to Lidia.

"There are so many beautiful places on this side. It's just that everything is complicated," says Lidia, as if sensing her discomfort. "Visiting these areas is enjoyable, at least this close to the border."

The girl walks with renewed energy, leading her quickly to San Babila, beyond the radiant jets of the fountain, then to Corso Venezia. The shops have enormous luminous signs that shine through the fog even from a distance, and the street is marked by fixed notices in the darkness, as far as the eye can see.

Lidia explains that, even though it can be dangerous at times, walking is one of her favorite activities. Irene listens and remains silent: the pressure of memory is crushing—*I used to like walking too*, she'd like to tell her, and instinctively thinks of turning around and going back. Instead she continues on, they keep walking, turning right, then left, until they reach the tree-lined walkway.

When they reach the gate, Lidia heads up the path. They pass a couple leaving, someone else passes them on their way in; the sound of electronic music comes clearly from the back.

"The villa is occupied," Lidia says, turning toward her. "I come here for a little company. You must have seen it plenty of times already."

Irene nods politely, and the girl shrugs, as if to say "I imagined so." They walk along the path until they reach the entrance to Villa Necchi and when they get to the main courtyard, Irene leans over to look into the swimming pool. Lying on the empty bottom are some boys around Lidia's age, their eyes closed, their arms relaxed at their sides; a piece with deep, repetitive bass notes drifts over the blue covering layer.

"I often imagine what it must have been like before," Lidia says, as they both walk toward the entrance. They climb the stairs and enter right after letting a rumpled man in his forties pass. At first glance, the interior seems identical to Irene's recollections—the wood, the banisters, the living room. She welcomes the sense of familiarity: for a moment she feels as if she's returning, not to the place but to a time. Swept up in the transport, she points to the kneeling statue in the center of the atrium, its face upturned to the ceiling.

"*L'amante morta*," she says, "*The Dead Lover*. That's the name of the sculpture."

"I didn't know that," Lidia says.

"The house was completed in 1935. In 2000 it passed to a government agency, which went bankrupt in 2025. The house was left uncared for, with the exception of volunteer organizations that tried to ensure its protection," Irene continues. "If it were on the other side, someone like me would have already sold it to a private individual. Maybe I myself would have handled the sale. I would have liked that."

"I'd be sorry if it belonged to someone and I couldn't come here," says Lidia.

"That won't ever happen. No one would buy in this area."

"Good." The girl walks to the left, toward the library. The armchairs have been replaced by metal chairs, the books and furnishings have disappeared. They pass some boys bent over laptop screens, one sitting at the desk, others on the floor, and Lidia heads confidently for the veranda.

"At this time of day, it's almost always free," the girl says in a low voice.

Irene lets Lidia go ahead of her. She notes the missing elements: the statues are gone, so are the paintings; the green marble is marred by large whitish patches, as if an acid had corroded its surface. Lidia settles on the sofa and for a moment Irene remains standing in front of her.

"What, aren't you going to sit?"

Irene sits down beside her. The sofa is the same as the one she recalls from the guided tours, the seat cushions now worn, yet in surprising condition considering the state's neglect. The girl slips off her shoes and rests her crossed legs on the cushions.

"I really like being here," she says, looking out. Beyond the glass panes of the veranda, the garden emerges from the fog as if caught in a drawn-out sleep.

"The last time I was here, you couldn't sit down," says Irene. "You weren't allowed to touch anything."

"And there wasn't any fog," adds Lidia. "At least not *this* fog."

“It was summer.”

“It’s summer now, too.”

“Touché,” Irene murmurs.

“It’s difficult for us,” says Lidia. “But I really can’t imagine how difficult it must be for you … those of you who saw everything the way it was before, you have memories that we don’t have to deal with. I imagine it’s easier if you’ve never experienced certain things, if you don’t know exactly what you’ve lost—”

“The sun is still there, outside the Po valley,” Irene interrupts her.

“But I want it here. It will never come back here again.”

“We don’t yet know if it will ever come back. It’s not scientifically proven.”

Lidia turns to her, looks at her as though for a moment she were the adult observing Irene from across the unbridgeable distance of sound, unassailable experience.

“It won’t come back during our lifetimes. That’s all that matters,” she says.

“Have you ever been anywhere else?” Irene asks, changing the subject.

“Yes, when I was very little,” Lidia replies. “Afterward there was no money to go on vacation anymore.” There’s no bitterness in her voice; she looks at the garden and seems to think of her childhood as if it were a story. “You’re not very interested in the subject, are you?” she adds.

“It’s not that,” Irene says, trying to relax.

“Does it bother you to talk about it?” Lidia asks, smiling at her.

Irene can’t help smiling back. Following Lidia’s

example, she too takes off her shoes, and sits with her legs curled up under her on the cushion, her hip up against the backrest. She looks at the girl for a long moment, but Lidia doesn't let it go.

"It doesn't bother me," Irene says. "I was very interested in the subject when I was young. I feel like it's too late to even talk about it now, that's all. A pointless misery."

The girl grows sad. Irene thinks about the flyer with the QR code she found in Lidia's bag the day she saw her in the shower. The link led to the sponsorship of a new virgin area in Northern Europe, a microclimatic bubble where it is still possible to savor the smell of unpolluted wind and water, a non-place which fires will not reach for the next twenty-five years at least. A privatized refuge, similar to the two others already present on the continent, accessible only to those who can afford the exorbitant costs of entering and purchasing a house.

Two or three years earlier, her parents had considered the idea of moving to a refuge, a suggestion that had foundered in the face of their children's resistance; neither Irene nor her two siblings had ever believed in the promise of areas of high climatic inviolability. And yet, the promotional brochure indicated photos and videos of clear streams and sunlight cascading through a forest's foliage. For a moment, Irene seems to see Lidia's dream with clarity: she can sense the doom of her intense desire, destined never to be realized.

Lidia sighs deeply, then looks out at the garden again. For a long while they remain silent, lulled by the sporadic sound of the voices of the boys in the other room.

"I wanted to thank you," Lidia says at some point. Her eyes are shining, and Irene tenses, unprepared. "Being able to stay in the house has meant a lot to me," the girl continues. "A great deal ... you can't begin to imagine ..."

The girl leans over and hugs her so impulsively that Irene doesn't have the presence of mind to stiffen. She holds Lidia close, gives in to the instinct to console her, stroke her. The contact with her body is unusual in the most endearing way.

"Thank you," Lidia murmurs, loosening her grip and sinking her head onto Irene's shoulder. "Can we stay here a little longer?" she asks.

"Of course," Irene replies.

Lidia straightens up and leans her head back on the sofa, cradled by Irene's arm.

"Tell me what this place was like before," the girl says. "Would you?"

"Sure."

"I wish I had your eyes, to see what you've seen. I wish I could borrow your head so I could remember it all," Lidia says, her cheeks flushed with a kind of euphoria.

Irene instinctively places a hand on her forehead, as if to calm her; she pulls it away immediately, but Lidia smiles at her, unperturbed. Irene tells her how it was, she spends at least an hour on the story, or maybe even more, the account goes on until the fog turns blue with impending dusk. Lidia listens in silence; a vein, visible from up close, throbs regularly under the smooth skin, at the edge of her temple. The same pulsation throbs in Irene's memory, in the only memory she does not verbalize. The crucial memory, entirely sensory, diluted in the didactic description, and in the minute exposition of the climate, the furnishings, the celebrated art elements: the troublesome thought of the body and the perception of its vitality in the legs and arms, being young as the fulfillment of the ideal form suitable for eternal life. Irene denies Lidia the most relevant truth, the one she feels pulsing in her own body, the electric charge destined to wither and fade: youth; feeling that one is immortal, seeing oneself as immortal, loving one's immortal self, and immediately afterward regressing to frailty.

The story tires her and, when it's time to head back, the darkness of the fog frightens Irene, who stays close to Lidia. The girl moves along without hesitation, leads her back to the border and then to the safety of Via Saterna. When it's time to say goodbye, Lidia stands at the door and watches Irene hurry away. Then she closes the door behind her and the house remains in darkness. Irene looks in the rearview mirror for a long time, waiting for a light to appear upstairs, until via Saterna dissolves around the first bend.

1985

Summer rewinds, and in the first week of September it seems about to start again, but the construction is complete, with most of the surface finishes already laid. They are waiting, and will be until mid-October, for the Calacatta marble.

All summer long the hibiscus in the garden has remained in bloom, a presence that alone manages to charge Lidia's enthusiasm in the morning or towards evening, at sunset. Her season is undoubtedly summer; since June, she has been nothing but positively joyful, or at least, so it's seemed to Dario. Often, especially in recent days, in the last couple of weeks, in the last few months, Dario doesn't know if the thought of Lidia's happiness corresponds to her as well or only to him. He is not always certain that what he convinces himself of is true: he measures his happiness on the basis of data extraneous to empathy. Of course, in the last two months, Lidia has wept, has said she was unhappy, has truly been unhappy and also anxious. She's vacillated, and her moods change quickly. There must be a whole stream of thought circulating in her silence, of which only the surface is visible. Despite her little crises, and her anxieties, Dario can't help but judge Lidia's joy by the complexion of her skin, by the way her body has moved this summer.

Dario often measures Lidia's joy with her youth; since he met her, it seems to him that he has suddenly come to fully realize his own age. Until the day he undressed Lidia, aging was an elusive concept. For years, he felt as if he had the same body, certainly not identical to that of his twenty-year-old self, but not so different either. In a certain sense his body continued to remain the same until the comparison with Lidia's. From that day on, he began to age, to be aware of the differences. In Saverio and in everything around him he can now see the sagging of the tissues, the shapes that the muscles lose and then alter, the way in which, in men between fifty and sixty, the stomach seems to separate from the chest, with intermediate spaces opening up like extraterrestrial creatures. Dario can see the future signs of decline even on himself.

In Lidia, on the other hand, the joy is undeniable, her face is all smooth, and her slenderness seems like a gift, as do the muscles that respond, the color of her areolas, her neck, seen from behind, the vertebrae flawless like chiseled crystal, and her long, thin hands; a light reverberates all through her skin. It is clear from Lidia's body that, once she reaches twenty, she will have to live forever, any other possibility is inconceivable. When he thinks about her, Dario's head spins, he always wants to look around for her, to see her with his eyes.

The laborers have abandoned the construction site for lunch; they will be gone for an hour or two, as they usually are. When there are other men around, Lidia always stays close to him, and if he isn't at the house she even chooses to go back to her mother. Dario knows that the workers scare her, make her feel uncomfortable. As soon as they leave, Lidia takes advantage of her newfound freedom to explore the house, check out the new elements. Since they started working on the interiors, every day seems to be a reason for excitement for her.

He sees her through the window, the glass superimposed on another glass, that of the outside veranda. From the center of the composition, Lidia moves to the left, walking across the garden, and when she reaches the far corner her figure divides into two reflections. Watching her, it seems impossible to Dario that he too was like that. Just a short time has passed, yet his best years have been consumed without him even noticing. Like having a diamond in your pocket for years, thinking it's a stone, then emptying the pocket along the way, leaving it on the ground. This thought in fact obsesses him. Lidia inflames him and at the same time dampens him, but on some days Dario can only keep telling himself that he wants to be rid of it forever, of this idea, of not knowing what to do. He quite often thinks about death.

He goes out to the garden, behind Lidia, turns on the outside faucet, crosses the lawn to the water pump. He picks up the bucket left in the shade of the boundary wall, and begins filling it. Lidia turns, drawn by the sound, and shields her eyes from the sun. For a moment she must have been afraid that the workers had returned, but now she smiles at him.

"What are you doing?"

"It's almost noon," Dario says.

Lidia joins him, leans against the ivy curtain covering the wall, and looks into the bucket, where the water becomes a white froth before rising to the rim.

"I have to show you something," Dario adds, checking his watch.

Lidia stands there watching him go back and forth from the garden to the living room, two, three full buckets of water, then the last one. When Dario returns with the empty bucket, she smiles at him.

"What?" she asks.

"Come with me."

She doesn't move away from the wall until Dario takes her by the wrist, his fingers stroking her forearm. In the meantime, the sun has reached its zenith. Dario makes Lidia turn around and covers her eyes. They shuffle backwards like crabs.

"I'm going to fall, wait, slow down."

They reach their destination when the sun has completed a perfect circle. The dark shape in the pool moves. Dario lets go of Lidia and says, "On the walls, look." She obeys. Around the circular staircase, the reflections of light on the water multiply and shift. Closer to the floor, the patterns are thin as blades—they expand up to the roof, faint, elongated specters.

"You remembered," Lidia breathes in a low voice. "But I only said it in passing, once ..."

Dario crosses his arms behind his back; his father always said that only those who have something to hide put their hands behind their back. Dario isn't sure who he's hiding from or what he's hiding. In recent days, in the last few years, his whole life has become a hiding place. Of course, Lidia's words had not gone unnoticed, it was only their third meeting, the first they'd had alone, and she had said exactly that, "the reflections of the water." Dario cannot now recall the conversation in its entirety, he only remembers that detail, "the reflections of the water," the memory that it had triggered: summer afternoons at the seashore, the reflections in the water that he so loved as a young boy, the hypnosis of the crystalline water on the sandy bottom. He associated a profound sense of happiness with that image, and Lidia with her brief remark had brought that same intense happiness to the surface. So there had to be a way, Dario told himself that day, to bring the reflections of water into a house.

"I remember," he says to Lidia.

From below, the sunlight's reverberation illuminates her like a spotlight, turns the white of her skin pale blue.

"I had them coat the bottom silver, so the reflections are bigger," adds Dario, looking away. "It works even without sunlight, with electric lighting. It's not as effective, of course."

Lidia may be moved, but Dario doesn't raise his eyes.

"I wanted the pool in the center. The center of a circular structure, see. In a sense, I would like this house to resemble the Anastasis of Constantine. Don't take me for a madman, or a megalomaniac, though maybe I am, it's almost essential to be one ... after all, there's a rock here too, a sepulcher and a resurrection. This is where the cornerstone is."

"Here?" asks Lidia.

"Yes. Underwater." Dario points to the pool. "The keystone, or quoin, is the stone that supports the entire building. Today we're celebrating it. The cornerstone is the foundation. I feel like I built the entire house in order to exalt just that one part of it. The entire construction is nothing but a justification for this focal point. Everything revolves around this center—the exterior, and even more so the interior."

When his voice, and the desire to speak, almost fail him, Lidia clings to him.

"All this is thanks to you, you allowed me to create the first significant project of my career. This house will make a profound difference, it will divide the before and after, you'll see. This house binds us together forever. I can't be apart from you for any reason; doing so would destroy me completely."

The following morning, Irene finds attorney Ferrari waiting for her at Via Saterna. The man is standing inside the gate, his hands clasped behind his back, distinguished in his gray suit, gazing pensively at the villa. Irene parks and wonders if he has already had a chance to discover Lidia's presence. She takes off her helmet, considers the best strategy to approach the subject, and tries to come up with a possible expedient that will enable her to avoid emerging weakened by the encounter.

"Good morning," she says to Ferrari, who nods to her. She enters the gate and joins him. "I wasn't expecting you."

"I know, apologies for the intrusion," says Ferrari. "A hearing was canceled and I couldn't resist, I wanted to see you at work. Besides, I haven't yet seen the house, you know? Only the floor plans."

"How long have you been waiting?"

"Not long. The gate lock will have to be fixed, it was open."

Irene takes the set of keys out of her pocket, careful not to betray her nervousness. "The locksmith will be coming next week," she says. "It's a pleasure to see you here. Follow me." Irene precedes the attorney along the path, and for a moment tries to formulate a reason to postpone the visit. She can't think fast enough, and curses herself for not having thought of this possibility, a risk that now seems to her to have been most likely from the beginning. She opens the door cautiously, afraid she will find Lidia waiting on the sofa. She suppresses a sigh of relief as she registers the girl's absence, then pretends to have trouble extracting the key from the lock, in order to detain the lawyer at the entrance, and give herself time for a quick glance at the living room. Lidia is nowhere in sight, she could be in another room or might appear at any moment. Irene goes to the veranda and throws open the nearest window. When she turns around, Ferrari has reached the pool: he raises his head and stares up at the skylight. If Lidia were to materialize on the stairs right now, they would be looking straight at one another. Irene remains petrified, waiting for the explosion, but Lidia does not appear. Incredulous, Irene clears her throat.

"Do you like it?" she asks Ferrari, in a loud voice, hoping that Lidia, if she is in the house, will realize that something is wrong and stay out of sight.

"Not at all," Ferrari replies.

"Really. It's a very beautiful house, in its own way," says Irene.

"The plan is pretentious, the choice of materials questionable, the design completely insane," the man adds. "If I were convinced that it was a beautiful house, I would not have hired you to sell it."

Irene forces a polite laugh.

"I'd like to take a tour," says Ferrari.

"It still hasn't been cleaned."

"It doesn't matter."

"The cleaning company is coming today, at nine thirty. Wouldn't you rather come back when I've got the furnishings in order?

"Thank you for your concern, but no," Ferrari replies, checking his wristwatch. "The likelihood that

I will have another free morning to come back here is remote. Will you lead the way?"

"Certainly."

Irene starts up the stairs, followed by the attorney, who takes the steps with caution, continuing to study the surroundings. He keeps looking down at the pool, as if wondering about its purpose. Irene walks him through the first floor, on the alert, ready to pick up the sound of Lidia's footsteps or see her suddenly emerge from behind the door of the next room. When they reach the second floor, and approach the green room, she's afraid she will find Lidia lying on the bed; the girl often sleeps there lately. The bed is undisturbed, however, the sheets covered with cellophane; the sink and shower in the pink bathroom are dry, wiped down, as if they too had never been used.

"Shall we continue up?" Ferrari asks, when they finish touring the second floor.

"There's only the attic up there."

"We've come this far."

Irene defers to the attorney, this time hurrying up the stairs and leaving him behind. When she gets to the top, she expects to see Lidia sprawled in the armchair where she first found her, but the girl isn't there. Relief doesn't keep her from wondering about her disappearance. Is Lidia really hiding?

"You see, it was worth it," Ferrari says, joining her. "It's stupendous, and the skylight ... magnificent.

"Magnificent," Irene repeats, distracted by thoughts of Lidia.

"So, are you already buzzing with excitement?"

"About what?"

"The auction, the sale," Ferrari says.

"No, not in the least," Irene replies.

"Have you considered the possibility of a fiasco?" the attorney asks.

"Why should I? It's not difficult to predict the outcome at this point. From my experience, I would say that it's also clear what kind of buyer will come forward."

"Extraordinary," Ferrari comments. "And what are your predictions based on?"

"The genius loci," says Irene.

"In the esoteric sense?"

"Pagan," Irene clarifies. "Don't get me wrong, the restoration of the spaces, the drafting of the informational materials, the selection of buyers—in all of this, a logical, mathematical principle prevails. But, when the time comes to sell, or rather, I should say, the time to buy, if rational organization has been observed, the buyer isn't aware of my intervention. This is why I always try, where possible, to recreate the original conditions. That's the reason for the photos and, even better, the three-dimensional projections: to replicate the memory of the building."

"And when might the 'genius loci' come into play?", the attorney asks.

"When the buyer is able to get in touch with the spirit of the house. Not a spirit in the strict sense, of course. I'm referring to the perception of the nature of the house, of the feeling with which it was built and then lived in. A communion with its original circumstances."

"I see," Ferrari says, then takes two steps towards the circular parapet and leans over, looking down. Irene joins him.

"I wonder what the person who built it had in mind," Ferrari muses.

"A temple," Irene replies. "A celebration. The house is austere in structure, sensual in its finishes. Some rooms seem to have been designed like jewel boxes, for example, the bathrooms on the first and second floors, the library, the green room, the verandas ... a compartmentalized and contradictory outcome. And yet, there is a strong motif that ties the whole together."

"And what would this motif be?"

"All the rooms were built around a non-standard scale of proportions. Perhaps you noticed the notes on the elevation, or the data on the plans: each measurement doubles, triples, or quadruples five feet five inches, or is one quarter or half of it. It's the golden ratio of this house. The scale of proportions is designed like Le Corbusier's Modulor, except that the reference is not the average human measurement, but a specific human measurement."

"Who was five feet five inches tall?" Ferrari looks at Irene as if she were leaving out the conclusion of the story.

"I have no idea," she replies, smiling. "I would guess it was a woman, but I haven't looked into it."

"Aren't you interested in the history of the house?"

"No. I never inquire about private homes for sale, except for data essential to the sale itself. Generally, the stories are sad."

"Very sensible. So the genius loci is in the measurements?"

"I don't know, what do you think? Maybe it's the circularity, infinity, immortality, the ouroboros ..."

"Must we not return and run down that other lane out before us, down that long, terrible lane ..." Ferrari recites, moving away from the parapet.

"Must we not return eternally?" Irene completes the quote.

"Well done, Sartori", says the attorney, clasping his hands behind his back. "I didn't take you for a Nietzschean."

Once again, they regard one another in silence for a few moments, won over by the test. Irene is relieved at the thought that Ferrari hasn't yet found out about Lidia. At this moment she realizes that she would be sorry to lose his esteem. There is something in him, in his posture and in the quality of his voice: an elegant inducement to offer the best of herself.

"Of course, it's not always clear what the genius loci is. I imagine the association will horrify you, but falling in love with a place follows the same rules as falling in love with a person: you perceive the essence and you choose. That's what motivates the buyer to assume the risk of the investment," Irene concludes.

"I find this building chilling," the lawyer admits.

"I'm confident that someone will fall in love with it precisely for that reason."

Suddenly, from downstairs, three loud knocks on the front door can be heard; Irene doesn't move, taken aback.

"You'd better go and open the door," the attorney says, moving aside to let her go first.

Irene checks her phone screen: it's almost nine thirty. It could be the cleaning company's crew; or Lidia, back from who knows where, assuming she ever left. On the way from the stairs to the door, she feels her hands getting cold, as if tension were causing the blood to drain from the body's peripheries. Ferrari follows her closely, and Irene has no choice but to open the door without hesitation. In front of them stands the figure of a small woman, a bleached blonde, wearing a dust-gray uniform with the company logo embroidered on the chest pocket.

"Good morning, we're from the cleaning service," she introduces herself, pointing to the van stopped in the middle of the street with its hazard lights flashing. "There are no parking spots, do you have a place where we can park?"

"I'm leaving," Ferrari speaks up. "My car is over there."

The woman thanks him and walks away down the drive.

"Thanks for coming," Irene says to the attorney.

"Keep up the great work. In fact, I think I'd like to come back to visit when it's all done. Before the sale, of course."

"Of course, whenever you like."

Ferrari says goodbye, and walks slowly toward the gate. Irene watches him get to his car and disappear behind the tinted windows, silently leaving Via Saterna.

When she's certain that Ferrari is gone, Irene spends a few minutes talking with the cleaning crew. She waits for Lidia to emerge from her hiding place, to turn up and say she was quick enough, alert enough, but the girl doesn't appear, and the workers scatter up the stairs. There are quite a few of them, they look at the house as if they were looking at a museum exhibit.

Irene looks for Lidia in the only areas she didn't look during Ferrari's inspection: she searches the kitchen, the cellar, checks the outer edge of the garden, goes up to the second floor, checks the narrow space under the bed, once again the attic. In a last attempt she goes out and walks the boundaries along Via Saterna, but Lidia isn't waiting, none of the shadows in the fog are hers.

Irene goes back; in front of the villa's wide-open gate, amid the hustle and bustle of industrious workers, she wonders where the girl may have gone, and when. And how you could possibly make every trace of yourself disappear so quickly, not leaving so much as a footprint behind. She tries to account for Lidia's belongings: she has never seen anything more than a few books, her boots, a clean change of clothes. She never wondered about what possessions the girl kept at Via Saterna, nor has she ever quantified them. Only now does she realize that the girl must have at least one other location in which to keep her clothes, her additional books, a laptop for studying. An emergency place where she can take refuge. She suddenly feels wary of everything she doesn't know about her. After a lengthy period of abeyance, suspicion returns, concern about the numerous unknown levels in which Lidia must live when she's not there in the house. When she isn't there? When she goes away? And for what reason?

Later, a general sense of guilt comes over her: Irene imagines that she made a mistake, that she must have scared the girl, and immediately afterward that Lidia is completely unreliable, or that maybe it was the visit to Villa Necchi the day before. Now Lidia's words come back to her, sounding foreboding: "I wanted to thank you, being able to stay has meant a lot to me." A casual comment that sounds like a goodbye. Irene questions her ability to read people, a task that has always been easy for her. How come she hadn't questioned herself then, after what Lidia said, how could she have disregarded the message?

In the early afternoon, while the cleaning crew is having lunch, Irene sits down on the sofa, which is finally immaculate. She's perspiring, her body leaning towards a desire that her thoughts find unappetizing—who should she have a child with? After all, didn't she dump Paolo like a sack of potatoes, denying him any explanation or reply? She blames her fogginess on the treatment, on the drugs—she is certain that she should stop taking them. The objectives of her decision are fraying.

"Where do we put the paintings?" asks one of the workers who have come to move the heaviest furniture from the cellar to the living room.

Irene rouses herself and consults her file of notes.

"Have you checked if the nails are secure?"

"Yes, we replaced some. We can start with the bigger ones before we go, if you want."

"Perfect, thanks," says Irene, following the man to the group of large paintings still covered in black cellophane. She watches closely as the wrapping is removed: the slashed openings first reveal three large Burri and Giacometti imitations, flaking forms in shades of white and blue, with intrusions of black. Irene recognizes the pieces seen in the projection: the two complementary paintings on the long wall to the right of the entrance door, and the third on the left, toward the dining table.

"The last one back there?" asks one of the workers, as he starts ripping the plastic off the bottom.

Irene looks at the sketches and notes again, unable to place the location. She doesn't remember noticing other paintings in the three-dimensional image. She moves toward the pool, looking for the spot the man indicated. She recognizes the symmetrical tips of two nails on the back wall, adjoining the staircase.

"Is it okay there?"

Irene nods and says, "Yes, if anything we'll move it later on."

She searches through the notes on her cell phone again, hoping to find a reliable reference, while the workmen hang the canvas. When she looks up again, she turns her attention to the painting: a carpet of gigantic dark-green foliage stands out against an opalescent sky. Amidst the greenery, which seems to be a surreal reproduction of water lily leaves, an adolescent figure sits cross-legged, her feet bare, wearing a white dress. The girl has dark hair that falls loosely behind her shoulders. One look at the face makes Irene freeze.

The two men walk away from the painting, and go back to clear the packaging away from the doorway. Irene slowly moves closer to the portrait, stopping at the edge of the pool. The girl in the picture watches her, her hands folded in her lap where the skirt of her dress enfolds them like a nest. For a moment, Irene thinks it's a hallucination. She keeps staring until the sounds around her fade. Someone closes the heavy door behind her, leaving her alone. Irene has no doubt: the lines of the portrait are precise, leaving no margin for error. The girl in the painting is Lidia.

1985

At the end of the day, Dario is often disoriented. Saverio is on his back, pushing him to finish the job, talking about other projects. Dario doesn't have the strength or the energy to admit that nothing else interests him—as if Via Saterna were his last job, and nothing should come after it, or before. He only comes to the studio in the late afternoon now, obligated to provide proof of progress. He has already failed to meet the completion deadline three times, but no one seems to care, certainly not Lidia, and not even Saverio.

Going home always depresses him a little, and in the evening Dario likes to walk. One evening, as he leaves the elegant building where the studio is located, he sees a man standing across the street. Not slowing down, Dario studies the stranger coming toward him, recognizing him only when he is a few steps away.

"Good evening, architect," the man greets him, blocking his path for a moment.

Lidia's fiancé has grown a beard since the last time they met, and he's lost weight. In any case, the original image is hazy, he hasn't seen him for at least five or six months. Dario briefly shakes his hand.

"This is a surprise. I would have gladly arranged a meeting."

"No problem. I was in the area and thought I'd stop by the studio to have a talk about the house. Do you mind?"

"Not at all."

"Which direction are you heading?"

"Cadorna."

"I'll walk with you."

The young man, who is really little more than a boy, explains that he recently returned from the United States. The assignment kept him away from Milan for the entire summer, he says, it was a fundamental step for his career. In New York, everything is bigger. Italy seems like what it is and perhaps will always be: a provincial outpost of the world.

"I went to see Via Saterna."

"And what do you think?" Dario asks.

Required to stop at a red light, they both end up looking at the traffic. Lidia's fiancé clasps his arms behind his back. He has the carriage of the children of the truly rich, the unshakeable composure, self-possessed even in an absurd circumstance like the one in which his appearance in front of the office has landed them. Dario doesn't think he has ever been like that; he lacks the genes for equanimity. He also knows he has no idea how to dress, or rather that he only knows how to dress by imitating others.

"It's all quite different from what we agreed on. I thought I had approved one project and rejected another, yet the house I didn't want was built."

Dario continues walking, and together they cross the street.

"It was Lidia's decision."

"Yes, she told me."

"What do you think of it?" The man seems to be reflecting, looking at the tips of their shoes in motion.

"I don't recognize anything resembling the house

I had imagined on Via Saterna. You must have wanted something so intensely that you produced a fixed image of it: it happened to me with this house. For five months, during the time I was away, I did nothing but think about what Via Saterna would be like when I returned, and all my speculations were based on the project I had approved. I thought about the design, even the draperies, I thought ... Maybe I've already told you that I have a passion for interior design. I had such a precise idea of the house, and I had nurtured such high expectations, that for a moment, when I saw Via Saterna, I didn't know where I was."

He speaks in an even tone, with no inflection, as if he were telling an acquaintance about an ordinary episode. There is no trace of fury in his voice, yet Dario feels uncomfortable.

"I'm sorry I didn't meet your expectations. In your absence, Lidia made every decision."

"Supported by you."

"Of course, supported by me. After all, the house is hers, and so are the funds."

"True, the house is Lidia's," the man nods. "But the project was ours."

They are halfway across Piazzale Cadorna, Ferrovie Nord Milano Station is lit up in the background. Dario interrupts the walk. "I'm sorry," he says.

"I don't like the house. I think it's ugly, the project is tasteless. But that's not important. The only important thing, you see, and the only reason I bothered to meet you at your office is to assure myself that you will not fail to take care of Lidia. She's a very fragile girl. I've known her for a number of years, I could say we grew up together, there is truly nothing more dear to me than her."

"I don't understand what you're saying."

"You have a family, sir. A wife and children. I sincerely hope you've thought about it before starting this relationship; it's not a fling. Lidia would have been happy with me. I've been by her side for many years and I would have taken care of her forever. Are you certain you can do the same?"

"I don't know what you're talking about."

"You have to swear to me that you won't hurt her."

"Have a good evening," Dario says, and walks away.

He has almost reached the opposite side of the piazza, when a hand wraps tightly around his arm. The man has followed him. His intense eyes are now desperate, very similar to his own, and the similarity makes Dario unexpectedly feel victorious. Despite his anxiety and fear, Dario suddenly realizes that he has prevailed—he's won.

"If you hurt her ..."

"Take your hands off me, you're making a fool of yourself."

"Please, I beg you. Let her go."

Dario pulls away from his grip, and for a moment it seems as if the man intends to strike him. Instead he hesitates, his hand still poised in the air. Dario turns his back to him, and the blow doesn't hit him until much later, remembering their few encounters: the arrogance with which Lidia's fiancé dismissed the ambitious plan for Via Saterna, the risk to which he exposed him with Saverio, a risk to which Dario had offered himself, from day one.

Irene slowly walks about the pool, tracing measured circles around the edge, taking her eyes off the painting only when it's unavoidable to avoid twisting unnaturally. Lidia is always there. Her identity is indisputable, it's impossible to mistake her even behind the adolescent features. She must be fourteen or fifteen years old in the portrait. The thick, wavy dark hair with its center part, the V-shaped peak that comes to a point at the hairline, the lowered eyes, silent and distant, and the vague, innocent, perennial expression of discontent are identical to their adult versions. The only difference is the skin tone; the painter invented a rosy tint, far from the anemic pallor of the real Lidia, or perhaps there were days when she was pale in a healthier way. For her too there must have been other seasons of youth.

Irene stops between the pool and the painting, now even closer. It is Lidia, in a portrait that has been in the cellar the entire time she and the girl have talked and worked together. A portrait ready to return to where it seems it has always been. Irene struggles to accept the evidence.

Instinctively, she taps the earpiece and calls Ferrari, still not sure what she should say. As the phone rings and rings, Irene imagines formulating a request for help in solving the enigma. The attorney doesn't answer.

Irene goes back to the sofa and perches on the edge, shifting the phone from hand to hand as if it were hot.

She tries calling Ferrari again without success. After the second failed attempt, she types "via saterna 7 milan owners" into Google, and the search engine responds with a series of links advertising the purchase of properties on Via Saterna, Milan, Castello Sforzesco, Milan Centro, Milan. A newspaper headline appears between the last pop-up ad and a link to court case records: "Tragedy in Affluent Milan: Young Woman Dies in Dramatic Fatality." Hunched over the screen, Irene waits for the article to load: a brief item from the news archive of 1986, about a dozen lines:

> *Friday night, what was supposed to be an evening of celebration among friends turned into a tragedy. Several young people, gathered at 7 Via Saterna, a prestigious address in the center of Milan, helplessly witnessed the accident that involved their host. The young woman, Lidia Castelli, twenty-one, fell from the stairs of the house in what appears to have been a dramatic fatality. Emergency response, which arrived promptly, was of no avail. Lidia Castelli was the heir of the late Tancredi, firstborn of the well-known Castelli family, a historic figure of Milan's wealthy class. The father, founding partner of the renowned legal consultancy firm Castelli and Associates, died prematurely in 1984 following a long illness, leaving behind his wife Elisabetta and their only daughter Lidia.*

The item is accompanied by two black-and-white photos, one beside the other: Via Saterna, deserted, photographed from the outside, and a photo of the victim. "Lidia Castelli" is written in small print, the girl posed in a blurry half-length shot, and Irene's hand starts shaking. It's Lidia, the same Lidia in the portrait, the same Lidia she knows.

Irene grabs her backpack and hugs the phone to her chest. There must be a rational explanation, she thinks, refusing to succumb to fear. And yet the eyes, the gaze of the girl who died in 1986 in a tragic accident, and the ID card in Lidia's purse ...

Feeling nauseous, she stands up slowly, as if afraid of being discovered—but by whom? Suddenly the idea of raising her head terrifies her, she has the sense that someone is looking at her. The force of that gaze makes her dash quickly to the front door. Those eyes behind her, watching her, staring, coming closer, the keys slippery in her hands. Irene manages to unlock the door, throws it open with a ragged breath, and the eyes are right there in front of her. The scream she thought she would let out dies in her throat. Lidia is standing there, dark-haired, eyes lowered, pale, looking up at her on the steps of Via Saterna.

"Can I come in?" she asks. The girl moves nearer, climbing the steps. She comes very close, hesitates for a moment, then squeezes in between Irene's body and the doorway, slowly, as if giving Irene the chance to keep her out. Irene doesn't move, and the girl glides past like water, leaving the impression of a warm body on her, the distinctive feel of living flesh. The irrational fear subsides.

"You found it," Lidia says. Behind her hangs her portrait, and the girl's gaze is duplicated in the twin reflection. "I thought about not coming back," she adds. "But I had no place to stay tonight."

"Who are you?" Irene asks, getting no answer. She maintains eye contact, moving closer: "Answer me!"

The girl backs away towards the pool, safe behind the obstacle of the sofa.

"This was my house," she says, her voice cracking. "My house." She seems to be having trouble breathing. She rubs her hands over her face as if waking up from a dream. "Don't come any closer," she says sharply, when Irene takes two steps toward her. She has a frantic look, which she immediately represses with an exercise in self-control. Taking a deep breath and relaxing her face, she retreats into a neutral expression while straightening her back and broadening her shoulders. She steps out of her own skin into another, and gives Irene a proud look: "I'm the daughter of the last owners," she says, in a clear, aloof tone. "I grew up in this house."

"The Kowalskis' daughter?" Irene asks uneasily.

"That's right."

Irene lets the information sink in. She should have foreseen it, or sensed it from the start. For a moment she considers the possibility that Lidia is lying, but the portrait is indisputable proof—there is no doubt that the girl is indeed her.

"I knew you'd find it today ... Yesterday, when I helped you move the paintings, I even thought about disposing of it, getting it out of the way ... but it's too big, too heavy, I couldn't move it. I also considered burning it, but I couldn't bring myself to do it. Anyway, what would have been the point, there's no way to avoid what's about to happen."

"Why did you lie to me?"

"Be honest, Irene," Lidia smiles. "Would you have

let me stay this long, if you'd known? I would instantly have become a much bigger problem than a homeless stranger."

"I don't understand. What's your objective? What do you hope to gain?"

"There's nothing to be gained," Lidia says. "I just wanted to stay here as long as possible, to put off the moment when I will have to leave it forever."

Irene looks away.

"Don't be angry," Lidia adds. "When it's time to go, I'll vanish without a word. I just need to stay as long as I can, until it's actually someone else's house, and I can never come back."

"I put my trust in you," Irene says.

"I'm sorry. I'm really so, so sorry ... I was scared." Lidia wraps her arms around herself. "You don't know how it feels. People like you don't have to live with this fear. You've always had a home, like your parents before you, you can't imagine what it means not to have a place to go back to, to know that the only home you ever had has been taken away from you, to feel so vulnerable, to know that you won't ever have another home—a place that belongs to you, for the rest of your life. Please, let me explain," Lidia says, moving closer. "I'll tell you the whole truth, I promise. I'll do anything."

Irene avoids her gaze, and in response Lidia kneels at her feet and puts her arms around her waist.

"Please, I don't want to sleep outside tonight," she leans her face into Irene and presses a cheek against her belly. "I'll do whatever you want, just let me explain."

Irene looks down at Lidia's forehead, a pale crescent

beneath the mass of her hair, her nose, and eyelids, the lashes squeezed tight on her stricken face. Her head gives off an intense heat that penetrates Irene's tissues and seems to spread inside, warming her. She feels the girl's hands clinging to her back, to her T-shirt, tightening until they reach her ribs; for a moment she wonders if this is how it would feel when ...

"Please, Irene."

Lidia looks up at her, rubbing her chin on Irene's abdomen, and Irene's fingers cup her face, caressing her forehead and then her head, following an improvised and precise path. The girl responds to the touch by burying her face against her, hugging her tighter. "Thank you," she hears her say. Her voice comes from deep within Irene, transmitted through her vocal cords. Thank you, thank you ...

Two years ago, after Irene's birthday celebration, her father had sat down next to her on the porch. They had left the chatty members of the family, her mother and sister, back in the dining room, busy talking about schools, private institutions, and the children's future college careers. Her father had crossed his legs and then, in an even tone, he explained to her that he had fallen ill. An aggressive form of arthritis, he said, localized in the cervical area. In a short time, the inflammation would attack and erode his joints to the point of preventing him from walking independently. Irene had looked at him—erect, composed, impeccable in his dark-green suit—and said that surely there had to be a treatment. Her father had smiled, giving her a quick glance of affection. "No, sweetheart, there is no treatment."

That day her father must have seen something in her: the ominous shadow of childhood, the fear of not having completed her evolution and of being abandoned.

The rare signs of endearment he had shown her punctuate her memory in an unerring diagnosis of his weak points: an inability to accept failure, a refusal to bend to the laws of nature, an unwillingness to fall short of the perfect ideal.

Now he stares into the fog, out beyond the terrace, his neck stretched forward. He probes the obscurity before them as if reading an omen. Irene joins him after lunch, sitting next to him on the wicker sofa. Ever since she returned to Milan, they have avoided each other after the tense encounter at dinner. Irene has deliberately been late to almost every meal, arriving right after his dose of sleeping pills, or just in time for his afternoon nap. From the onset of his malady, her father has had a much greater need to sit still, to pause at times where in the past it would have been impossible for him to do so.

"Sometimes I feel like someone is sawing my head off my neck, bit by bit, a little more every day," he replies, impassive. "Where is your mother?"

"On the phone with Ettore," Irene says. "He arrived in Antarctica this morning."

Irene runs a finger over her thigh, along the outside seam of her pants, and strains to imagine an alternative conversation between father and daughter, a kind of normality that is not exactly normal but in any case different from the war games that neither of them can give up.

"How's the house going?" he asks, after a few minutes of silence.

"Good.

"How much? Seven, eight?"

"At least thirteen."

"Don't be absurd. Ten at most."

"Thirteen at a minimum."

"How long has it been since you last worked in this market?

"I might even say fourteen, I'm certain of it."

"The market is in decline."

"Not mine."

"Your *what?*"

"*My* market doesn't suffer downturns. Buyers of properties like this can only become wealthier. You know it's not about houses, but accessories, luxury extravagances."

"What's the address, did you say?" her father persists.

"Number 7 Via Saterna. Castello area."

"Yes, I know where you mean. But I can't remember the house. Who handled it?"

"Studio Esadea."

"Esadea?"

"Yes. They worked in Lombardy in the 1980s, mainly in the commercial sector. They closed in 1987."

"Well, in fact I don't remember them," her father comments dismissively. "You don't even have the name of a renowned studio to sell, at most you'll close at nine."

"You haven't seen it. It's a unique work, one-of-a-kind."

"*One-of-a-kind* doesn't mean anything. Nothing *one-of-a-kind* has been built around here in the last fifty years."

"Trust me, you should see it."

"I've already seen everything there is to see."

"That's not possible, Dad." Irene leans back, stretching an arm behind her back. "Nobody has ever seen *everything there is to see.*"

He remains silent for a few minutes, then straightens up.

"Okay, okay," he says. "Take me."

"What?"

"Take me to see the house," her father turns to her, accompanying the order with a challenging look. "While your mother is out. On Sunday mornings she has mass, then lunch with her friends. We'll take my car."

"You've never wanted to go anywhere with me," Irene can't resist the urge to provoke him.

"I never go out. I'm desperate and prepared to accept it."

Irene is silent and they both stare into the fog again, contemplating from memory the invisible view of the horizon. She thinks about Lidia, about her words: she listened to the story just as it was told to her, or rather poured out to her. It seems to her that, out of nowhere, Lidia's life found her and imploded in her, rubble from a future that has already happened. "I have to take you somewhere," the girl had concluded her story, just when it seemed that her voice had become one with the walls of Via Saterna. *Where?* Irene wonders now, her eyes searching the unvarying mist outside, and immediately the illumination hits her: just like her father, she is not observing, but asking a question. And just as it does to him, the question paralyzes her, forcing her eyes to scan through an incomprehensible language—is a place still a place if you can't see it?

1985

The completion of the work on Via Saterna, or the awareness of its completion and conclusion, come to Dario in mid-summer, as a revelation. One Wednesday afternoon, before dusk, Lidia slips her bag off her shoulder and drops it on the floor. There are no furnishings and fixtures yet, they have only visualized them, browsed through catalogues and selected them, but the search has been so intense and extensive that it's as if the house were already fully appointed. They often move about following the phantom boundaries of beds and tables, armchairs, and two of their favorite rooms, the bathrooms on the second floor, are already equipped. Lidia has just set out a supply of towels, a domestic gesture that prompts a glimpse of the overall vision. Seeing the overall vision is an ability that Dario feels he has lacked since his studies, the reason why it is difficult for him to gain professional acknowledgment. His most brilliant colleagues always seem to start from the whole, but he instead can only start from the individual part, an accumulation of single parts. The obsessive tenacity to individual details and their accrual are his hallmark: a method that Saverio, and everyone else, considers risky and foolish.

Even with Via Saterna, Dario was unable to escape the law of details. He started with water, the circular walls, and everything else grew around it, apparently of its own volition. Often, especially during the design stage, he considers his method brilliant, and convinces himself that he is special. And sometimes even after the work is completed, or when he is able to accept that it is completed, the overall vision reveals itself to him unexpectedly. Today Lidia walks through the overall picture, and for a moment Dario is able to see clearly: the house is finished, and it is finished now, despite everything that still needs to be done.

Lidia too seems to come to the same awareness. She looks around with her arms crossed over her chest, clasping her elbows, and circles the empty pool. She still doesn't know what its purpose is, but she doesn't ask; she waits.

"What do you think?" Dario says, joining her.

Lidia looks up toward the skylight.

"You know what I think. Right now, in fact, I don't feel worthy of this house, or rather, this is the first time I've thought that: it's too beautiful, magnificent. In the sense of grandiose."

"It's your house. It resembles you."

Lidia smiles, not looking at him. She goes back, picks up her bag, heads up the stairs, and Dario, right behind her as they go up, sees her undo one of the buttons along the side of her white skirt, as if to make herself more comfortable, as if he were not right behind her. From that perspective he watches her proceed along the second floor corridor, through the custom-made doors: the play of proportions is wholly erotic, heavy and dense, the further they advance the more viscous it becomes. Lidia undresses, drops her clothes on the floor, Dario thinks that the green of the walls will have to be glazed, the glaze will reflect the light better, the light will make the skin look like marble, even if glaze is never done in a bedroom, it doesn't matter. Lidia takes some folded papers from her bag, then a fountain pen that must have belonged to her father; it has the look of an item stolen from an unused writing desk. Dario watches her spread the papers on the floor, at his feet. She hands him the fountain pen.

"What's this?"

"You have to sign."

"What is it?"

"It's half of your house. All this."

Dario understands only when Lidia nods toward him and then toward the walls, a grand gesture for an audience—the audience present at the discussions she must have had alone, with herself, the doubts, the unanswered questions.

"I can't."

"You have to, because I want it this way."

"You don't realize. You can't make these decisions on the spot, you can't let yourself get carried away."

"Listen," says Lidia, "this decision was made a long time ago, maybe the first or at most the second day I saw you, when we spoke to each other. I know you believe this too, and the house is mine, my father left everything to me, if I wanted to have it demolished and rebuilt, I could ask to have it done, it could happen at any time—haven't you ever suddenly realized that you had the right to choose? I'm sure it's happened to you too, at least once, maybe the first day or so we met. This is merely a formality, it's my gift; it's me, I no longer belong to anyone. I broke off the engagement. I ended it last night. There won't be a wedding next year, no family—certainly not that one. That's right, last night. The engagement is off."

Lidia tightens his hand around the fountain pen. Dario can't think of anything other than the green glaze on the walls, and Lidia's skin as she sleeps, with the reflection of an opal, an image that is immediately an aesthetic project. Lidia has broken off the engagement and will no longer be getting married: instinctively, the idea seems terrifying.

"See, it's not difficult," she continues, "but to sign you have to get on your knees. I'll stand here." Dario obeys, kneels on the floor, and leans forward; at Lidia's feet, he signs the contract by which she gives him half of the property. "Now you own half of me," she says when he has finished signing, gently guiding his head between her closed thighs and pressing his mouth against her sex: you choose which, as below, so above.

They had become poor very quickly, Lidia had told her, but her parents hadn't been able to explain it to her. The speed with which the world around them crumbled had hit her with a delayed effect, years later. A series of unforeseeable events had been triggered, as her father had said, before they attempted to flee to South America: one misfortune had caused two more and those two four and so on, until it became impossible to remedy. Only her mother had managed to escape: she, the owner of half the assets and half the debts, chose Northern Europe. Once there, she had disappeared without a trace. At sixteen, tired of waiting for a phone call that would never come, Lidia had thrown her cell phone into the Idroscalo, Milan's artificial lake. The only family asset remaining in her possession, it too was on the list of lines monitored by the Guardia di Finanza.

There had been no crisis, of course. Her father had been born rich and had no perception of risk. Both of them, her mother and her father, depended on the good life like those who have never known any other kind. Faced with the functional shrinkage of their assets, neither of them had been able to deal with the idea of downsizing. All they would have had to do was sell and stop buying, to settle for what, in any case, would have been more comfortable than the totality of lives that Lidia had encountered in her subsequent existence, the experience of being poor.

"When we were rich, I was too young to realize it.

And by the time I was old enough to understand, we hadn't been rich for a long time." Lidia had said that with a shrug, perhaps reciting from memory the most tolerable version of the story, the one in which the least possible had been taken from her. Irene repeats the words to herself, one by one, even this morning as Lidia is walking just in front of her, at her side but two steps ahead. She asked her to accompany her somewhere, but she wouldn't say where, as if Irene had to trust her. Trusting, she followed her.

On the subway, Lidia grabs the zipper of Irene's jacket and zips it up to the top, under her throat, covering the gold necklace.

"Where are we going?" Irene asks.

"Somewhere quiet," the girl replies. "But first we have to go through the station."

Irene observes the faces, overexposed in the neon lights. When it's time to search the car they're traveling in, she lets them push her without offering resistance. When they reach the stop for Stazione Centrale, Lidia quickly slips through the crowd in front of her. The underground passages are seething with masses of people moving through, the junctions between the hubs to change lines are clogged.

"To the left," Lidia says, turning for a moment and peeling off in the direction of the stairs.

"What?" The AI-generated voice, followed by the shrill sound of the whistle, announces the stop. Irene doesn't understand.

"Here!" Lidia repeats, quickly waving her over.

The tide of exiting passengers engulfs them, separating them. Irene starts to follow the girl, but the mob closes around her, pushing in the opposite direction. She loses her footing, tilting backwards.

"Excuse me," she says, struggling to straighten up. "Sorry."

No one seems to have heard her; the crowd surges ahead like an immense corpus toward the platform behind her. Irene leans forward, looks for Lidia, but all she sees around her are faces hidden by masks, balaclavas, or watch caps, the fleeting glimpse of an eye, a tuft of hair. She feels her face flush, her heartbeat accelerate, panic closing her throat. Then someone firmly grips her wrist.

"This way," Lidia shouts, re-emerging from the crowd, yanking her arm. The girl elbows her way forward, making room, aggressively breaking through the flow. She manages to lead her to the escalators, bringing her to safety. She looks at Irene, who is dazed and breathing heavily. "You never go on the metro, do you?" Lidia asks, opening the top button of her jacket.

Irene shakes her head, looking down. As the next train is announced, another horde of travelers descends on the platform gaining the few seconds needed to change lines.

"Never get caught in the middle. They're like rip currents out at sea." Lidia follows her gaze.

Irene turns around, nauseated by the turbulent throng, regretting her decision: they're already in the station's interstellar gate, identical to the one she saw in the renderings of Expo 2025. It's been ten years, maybe more, since she's traveled by train.

"I come here almost every morning," Lidia explains.

They move on at a brisk pace, taking a couple of different stairs, until they reach one of the lower floors.

"What do you come here for?" asks Irene, looking around.

Shadowy figures stand in front of digital screens at the kiosks and wait in line for cigarettes. Further ahead, those who aren't waiting for something move quickly, filling the main passageways. Lidia sidles behind the columns, slips through the turnstiles, retracing a route scored by habit. Irene follows behind her, watchful. They are stopped by the line for the checkroom.

"I have some stuff here," the girl says, putting her hands in her pockets. The line is full of people without suitcases, many seem to be the same age as Lidia, some are slightly older or younger. "It's difficult to carry your stuff with you, especially if you change places often, if you don't have a base, let's say," Lidia explains. "All my things are here at the storage room. Downstairs there are a couple of self-service laundries and the bathrooms. Although, for washing, the public swimming pools are better."

The girl's words describe the variables of a well-tested process that has become natural: an equation that is repeated together with its result. Irene conceals her embarrassment, scanning the faces in front of them, all of them illuminated by the blue displays of their phones or notepads. "Most of them are college students," Lidia says, intercepting her questions.

They remain silent as the line flows along smoothly. When they reach the window, they claim a key.

"Come on," Lidia says, moving confidently toward the back of the checkroom, where a series of metal lockers are jammed together.

The girl unlocks number 15, revealing a stack of books balanced precariously on a pile of clothes. She pulls a sweater and a pair of black pants from the pile, holding the books in place with one hand, then quickly undresses. Irene stands between her and the entrance, covering Lidia as the old clothes are replaced with fresh ones.

"No one notices," the girl protests.

Irene looks away again, feeling as if she's crossed a private boundary that she should never have been allowed to.

"Okay, let's go," Lidia slams the locker shut, unfazed.

"Where?"

"Up to the street."

When they emerge from the last escalator leading to the exit, Lidia and Irene look out over the piazza, protected by the colonnade. Out of the fog, the wail of the audible traffic signals rises in a mournful lament, accompanied by the flickers of stick-on lights, flash lights, and reflectors affixed to backs and legs, and LED headlights mounted on the frames of electric vehicles.

"Let's follow a piece of the course," Lidia says, pointing to the illuminated path starting in front of them to indicate the pedestrian crossings in the piazza.

"My father was arrested," the girl had said at a certain point in her account. She also said that, nine or ten months after being placed in a foster home, she almost believed she had removed her parents from her memories, as if they had never existed. Her mother had left her no tactile memories, had never cuddled her or held her, and soon Lidia was no longer able to even remember her smell. Her father, on the other hand, had survived, troublesome, tenacious, affectionate as he was with everyone, impulsively indiscriminate. He gave of himself without thinking of the possibility of, one day, having nothing left to give. Lidia never went to see him, in prison. Bitterness is an ugly thing, she said.

They walk on, following the blinking routes marked along the street. Irene feels vulnerable. Passers-by emerge from the fog when they are already quite close, and the acoustic jumble slows her reflexes. Lidia tilts her head back, and takes a deep, relaxed breath, like someone who is in her element. "I love my father very much, but I never want to see him again."

They don't walk very far. Ten minutes after leaving the station behind, Lidia leads her off the path, away from the din of the main thoroughfare. They walk among the flowerbeds for another five or six hundred yards, avoiding the gray shapes of the trees, until they reach what seems to be a large, paved area closed to traffic.

"We're here," Lidia announces, moving straight ahead. A monumental profile of white marble emerges from the fog: Irene recognizes the Famedio. Lidia stops at the foot of the staircase, one foot already on the first step. "Do you like cemeteries?"

The figure of a woman dressed in black with a bunch of white roses clutched in her hand breaks through the opaque wall in front of them, and walks in silence before disappearing at the top of the stairs, swallowed up by the main entrance.

"Yes," Irene replies, sincerely.

"Me too," the girl says, starting up the steps.

Irene follows her. She feels dazed, as if Lidia were

ferrying her into a dream; she thinks of the work to be done, the repairs and the forms to complete, the advertising for the opening of the next auction, and all of that, all the encumbrances of the real world, all of it suddenly seems incomprehensible to her. They move inside, where the resounding noises from the street seem distorted, as if from another planet.

"I've been coming here often, for a couple of years," Lidia says, walking around Manzoni's sarcophagus. "It relaxes me."

"I liked cemeteries, too, when I was your age," Irene says.

"When you were my age?" Lidia smiles knowingly.

"That's right. The older you get, the less enjoyable it is."

"But you're still very young."

Irene shakes her head without replying, as they pass the statues in the portico. They go down more stairs, emerging into the inner court, reserved for outdoor crypts. Irene savors the heavy, unbroken silence and the fog that hovers over the yews and cedars. It's clear what kind of relaxation Lidia is talking about: an awareness of the lack of activity, or the evident superiority of non-human activity, in plants, underground, a renunciation of the tension of survival.

"When was it that you returned home? You haven't yet told me," Irene says, as they walk along the central path heading towards the back.

"Two years ago." Lidia gestures for her to follow her to the right, proceeding among the tombs. "When I came of age, my foster care ended. I had worked, I had saved up some money to come back to the city and start university, but I had no luck finding accommodations.

Most of the rooms were too expensive, and several times I ended up being evicted because the landlord had found someone who offered more money. For a while I would go and look at Via Saterna from the street. It was the first thing I did when I left the foster home. The villa had remained closed up for a very long time. Maybe no one wanted to take a look at it, buy it, I have no idea: you would certainly know more about that than me. In a dark period, I was in danger of ending up in the encampments, in the south. I didn't seem to have any alternatives. Then, one evening, I thought that on the whole my life was already at risk, and that the worst that could happen to me was to be arrested. The idea of spending a little time in the same place and being able to study, whether in a cell or finally back at home again, was compelling. In the end, no one arrested me, and I managed to get in; the key to the porch was in the same place where the cleaning lady always left it. So, taking a few precautions, I returned."

The girl slows down, her eyes searching for something. She sees what she's looking for, and Irene follows her. They stop at the foot of a large rectangular tomb, very close to the entrance of a crypt.

"It was when I came back to live on Via Saterna that I found out about her. It happened while I was looking for ads about the sale of the house: one of the results contained information about her death."

The marble relief emerges from the smooth surface of the tombstone like a body rising from water. The hands are sculpted to cover the eyes, the mouth is closed and the forehead smooth, the hair spreads out, drifting beyond the corners of the slab. The body is naked, petite, small breasts, narrow pelvis, the pudenda covered by a fabric that drapes around the legs. The feet, exposed like those of a lifeless Christ, appear to be glazed with a thin veil of clear, white skin. Irene reads the inscription lower down, behind the sculpture's head: Lidia Castelli 1966–1986.

Irene struggles to appear impassive. "What's your real name?"

The girl traces a semicircle in the gravel with the toe of her boot, then approaches the tomb, giving her a sidelong look.

"That name no longer exists," she says, standing on the gravestone.

"What are you doing?" Irene protests.

Lidia lies down next to the sculpture, crossing her legs and arms as if preparing for a nap.

Irene looks around, afraid the caretaker might appear. "You can't!" she says to the girl.

Lidia looks up at her, seraphic, not at all intimidated. "You should relax."

"It's inappropriate."

"I come here all the time, I don't do any harm. I'm a very respectful visitor."

"It's childish."

"Do you want to continue your tirade or do you want to hear what I have to tell you?"

"What if someone comes?"

"Irene, no one will come," Lidia says, grumbling. "Sit here."

Irene hesitates, as the girl pats the marble with the palm of her hand. The silence persists around them: no approaching footsteps can be heard, no alarms sound, and she gives in to the invitation, sitting on the cold edge of the tombstone.

"Thank you," Lidia says, then clears her throat. "As I was saying, I come here often."

"If you lie down next to her," she says, "you realize what death is, or at least I think I do, because apart from the leaves of this tree over her grave there is nothing, you see nothing, only the milky void that never changes. Every now and then you think you can make out the sun in the fog, but even that is an irrelevant occurrence, and any sound is the repetition of what precedes it. I don't think my parents knew that someone had died in the house they had bought and chosen as the family home. If she had known, my mother would never have set foot in there. Maybe this was something that was talked about among the neighbors, but my parents didn't associate with neighbors, or even many people from around the city: my father and mother had exotic tastes in friendships.

"It seems to me," Lidia continues, "that, up until a certain age, I had done nothing but store up information, that as a child I had been a tape recorder with a built-in countdown. When I grew up, that is, when my parents lost everything and my life as I knew it was destroyed, I began to understand; every detail registered by my eyes, my nose, my memory, came back full of significance, totally understandable. I saw the disaster approaching after it was already done. My father bet on the stock market the way any father would gamble at cards, more and more, higher and higher, until he started selling our things. *Our* things, mine and my mother's. The houses, the boats, the jewelry. When the televisions, cell phones, and laptops disappeared, my mother realized what was happening. Still, I don't think the extent of the disaster was clear to her either, at least not until it was too late. We were two little girls, my father had sold himself as the adult of the house—we trusted him.

"When I was able to return, I explored the villa as I had never done before. That's how I found the ID card: it was in a jewelry box, in the cellar. The idea that someone had died in the same place that was the happiest for me, the place I would always want to return to, has never bothered me. Do you think death is a bad omen? Sometimes I've wondered. Maybe no one can be happy in a house where someone has died. Like a curse. What do you think? Gothic but credible.

"After my parents abandoned me, I stopped using my name. I borrowed hers. Since I no longer have a home, I am nobody. And of course, I've learned that this category is full of people. Then again, I was never able to enjoy wealth. I can only imagine what it would have been like, what it would have meant for me to have a safe haven. Instead I'm left with a memory that's impossible to erase, resistant to the tabula rasa of the last seven years: the warm feeling of taking off your clothes and putting on fresh ones, folding your shirts and pants on the bed, waking up in the same room every morning, day after day, learning by heart the light, the comfort, the shadows, predicting the temperatures. Another persistent ache is the idea of having grown up within those walls. You see, regardless of the outcome, there's no doubt that there was love in my family, even if only for an instant, something that warmed me so deeply, only there in that place, in the house that my parents lost, that they thoughtlessly let go.

"The future is so frightening without a home. As much as I am resigned, as much as I am aware of being part of my generation's inevitable downturn, and as clear as it is that an untold number of us, millions of individuals at the height of their potential, in the prime of life, will never be able to afford a house, as much as the tedious refrain of flexibility, sharing, rejection of bourgeois tradition, autonomy, freedom to travel, to move about, aims to make us feel less alone, less adrift, part of a group of millions of individuals ready to break away, as much as our youth is described to us as an indisputable gift, I feel I have lost everything. I say this serenely, with no rancor, having made my peace, because it was inevitable: we have lost everything."

1985

Since Carla and the children have been away, since Lidia's mother and boyfriend also left Milan for the summer, time and space have dissolved. The city is suddenly different, it has transformed into a detached location, as if the distance from any glances has made them invisible. They wander through the night, aimlessly.

Often, in the evening, Lidia wears short, backless dresses and sheer stockings. As he drives, Dario observes the recess of her knees and the burnished turn of her thighs. In the last month, they have gotten into the habit of frequenting the same places where Lidia's friends meet: they are discreet people, they don't talk, they don't ask questions, they have seen things far more remarkable than an engaged woman with a possible lover. Lidia and Dario try to be careful, when they don't drink, but often they drink and don't remember. When Lidia is tired of dancing, they drive until dawn, and for a moment Dario thinks about the risk of losing everything. That someone might see him, that his wife might find out, that the marriage might blow up. Even so, for a number of weeks he's been indifferent to this risk.

Their favorite activity—Dario's favorite activity with which Lidia willingly goes along—is wandering around construction sites. Private and public buildings, megastructures and simple renovations are everywhere, all sizes and styles, for all purposes. The density of scaffolding, fences and cranes is unbelievable, metallic clusters flourishing at the edges of streets or around the empty craters of foundations.

We live in an extraordinary time, Dario tells Lidia, and she too seems to be excited by the idea of expansion, a hunger for growth, spreading out in all directions, simply because it's possible, because it can be done. Along with the construction sites flows the thought of money, and anything extraneous, any object or concept unrelated to the capitalization of resources, pales. It's impossible to establish what is important in the world: the time that Dario spends with Lidia, Via Saterna, the construction, it's all there, the future compressed into a timeless expanded present.

One night, exhilarated about the installation of the skylight, Lidia starts feeding a few hundred thousand-lira bills into her Alexander shredder and manages to get through a good portion of them before Dario can stop her. Later, in the empty house, she asks him to fuck her on the floor, where the flooring is still just an area of dust and crushed stones: she says the pain under her hands and knees helps her breathe and enjoy it more intensely. She spends days afterward plucking the slivers of stone out of her skin. They celebrate with the same ritual at each tiny step forward, until all the joints have been welded.

At the Tuesday meeting, Valentina, Adora's treatment coordinator, wears a blue silk shirt so ethereal that it makes her look like an anthropomorphic artificial intelligence. Irene informs her that she has changed her mind about the fertilization process, by imagining that she is talking to her computer. The trick works, she is able to recite her requests in a very precise order, in accordance with a visual mind map, without listening to herself. At the end of the meeting, Valentina emails her a psycho-attitudinal questionnaire and donor catalog, reminding her that, once she has made her choice, she will only need twelve days of final therapy before proceeding with the insemination. Irene scans through the selection of compatible donors, a list of somatic traits, measurements, psycho-attitudinal test summaries, childhood and adult life photos to guarantee the result. The voice recordings, handwriting samples, interests, all the particulars play a part in the calculation of probabilities and hypotheses, and Irene imagines herself holding a child in her arms, projecting the idea of her voice into affectionate approval or authoritative instruction. For long moments she sees herself gazing at her son or daughter, feeling moved and lost in thought. The anticipation of motherhood is an undercurrent throbbing beneath the controlled processes, along with the thought of Lidia.

*

The following day, on Via Saterna, Irene finds Lidia waiting for her in the garden. The girl is walking along the outer perimeter, following the horseshoe-shape edge of the veranda, so absorbed that, for a moment, Irene is afraid she has interrupted something. Then Lidia waves her over.

"I'm going over a lesson," she says, greeting her.

"I don't want to disturb you."

"You're not disturbing me. What's the plan for today?" Lidia reaches out, slips off Irene's fog glasses, then puts them on herself and looks up.

"They don't work like that," Irene says.

"Who says so?"

"They track heat sources."

"There's a swallow flying overhead."

"I didn't think they flew here anymore."

"They don't fly anywhere anymore, they're almost extinct," Lidia says, taking off the glasses and handing them to her. "Take a look."

Irene puts them on, looking where Lidia points.

"Over there." Lidia stands next to her and gently guides Irene's chin to move her face in the right direction.

"I don't see anything."

"Are you sure?" The girl leans in, her hair brushing Irene's temple.

"I'm sure."

Lidia removes Irene's glasses for her. "Never mind," she says, "it must have flown away. Let's take it as a good omen."

"For Virgil, swallows are harbingers of death. Did you know that?" Irene can't resist the temptation to needle her.

"And who might this Virgil be?" Lidia laughs, going

back into the house. "So then, what do we need to do today?"

Irene takes the camera out of her backpack as the girl watches attentively.

"The background is complete. We have to take photos."

"What will they be used for?"

"The announcement of the auction."

Lidia watches in silence as Irene adjusts the camera settings, focuses on the wall behind her, takes the shot, then another. "Where do you want to start?" she asks, when Irene is ready. "I think we should start with the attic."

Irene frames the girl as she moves toward the stairs, immortalizing her against the light, and Lidia gives her a knowing look as she leads the way. On the screen, her figure appears as a black and ivory stream, as if she really were the ghost Irene had believed in for a moment. Instead Lidia exists in the undeniable material form that walks in front of her. Her body leaves a trail, and it is the body that Irene thinks about more and more often, since she read the qualifying questionnaire. She is certain that it is a question of formality, and precisely because the questions will not constitute the basis for a value judgment, it seems to her that they strike deeper, that they are in some way more pregnant in offering an authentic portrait. The questions aimed at reconstructing a profile of her affective life, of her education and upbringing, the aptitude to undergo a treatment responsive to the demands of a new life, everything makes her think of Lidia as a testimonial to failed nurturing. Just as she imagines herself as a mother, in a variety of projections and words spoken to herself, she thinks of Lidia as a child, and the two tracks are superimposed. The future in which Irene will be a mother is the past in which Lidia was abandoned.

When they reach the attic, the girl helps her open and close the windows, choosing the prevalence of this or that light, as if tricks were actually needed. Via Saterna appears restored to the splendor it has never known, just as it must have been conceived by its designer. Irene captures a shot of Lidia's feet, bare on the dark parquet. The girl lets her work in silence; with each passing minute, the quiet becomes ceremonial.

Irene lets Lidia lead her even when she knows that the trajectory follows criteria other than the logical visiting order. Not clockwise or counterclockwise, nor even according to a principle of contiguity or succession. The girl proceeds from the top to the first floor and from the first to the ground floor. Irene is soon struck by the idea that the routes are chosen from memory. Lidia progresses gingerly, replicating explorations made on an idle afternoon, coming and going, moving along the temporal traces of her previous life. Behind her, Irene takes shots where the girl's gaze pauses devotedly, sure of her intuition. Suddenly, the task is emptied of its official purpose and filled with another; on impulse, spontaneously, they work together on a reconstruction, a commemoration.

Lidia tells her story wordlessly and, at the end of the last chapter, leads Irene to the heart of the memory: the green room, where she has taken refuge in the last few months, collecting under the bed those essential items indispensable even when faced with an abrupt flight.

After discovering the truth, Irene no longer has the fortitude to investigate. She sees the girl bend down and hastily shove something into the hiding place, several times, nesting like an unlawful squatter in the place where she should have been at home. Setting aside her suspicions, Irene can't help but feel good: feeling good is worth ten times as much as the exercise of any authority, because she is certain that Lidia has noticed her clemency.

The girl doesn't wait for Irene to finish shooting pictures of the room, she flops onto the silk bedspread, relaxing as if after a long day's work. *I'm exhausted*, her eyes seem to say, when Irene approaches the bed.

Lidia sprawls on her back, arms outstretched on the pillow.

"Aren't you going to take a picture of me?" she smiles.

Irene obeys, framing half of her face. Lidia promptly turns on her side, leaving her bare shoulders captured in the photograph. She gives Irene a sidelong glance, pleased at having eluded her. "Aren't you tired?"

Irene walks around the bed warily, sits down on the opposite side, and rests her back against the headboard, arching her spine. "Yes, I'm tired."

The girl watches her for a few moments, then slides closer, rustling the fabric, and rests her head on her lap. She looks at her, studying her as Irene imagines she would study samples of plants.

"Are we done, then?" Lidia says.

"Yes."

"It doesn't seem real," the girl continues. "But there are so many things that I thought could never or would never happen, and yet ..."

Her body is curled up tensely, and the smooth lines of her muscles are visible under her clothes: a white T-shirt, and a pair of cotton pants. The bones stand out more sharply than the muscles, the framework is distinguishable, and Irene feels as if she's in a privileged position from which to view a carved ivory chest from a distant country. She takes in all the details, the accented adherence to the joint knots, the neck triangle, the silky shine of her hair; she recognizes the almost irresistible need to sink her hands into Lidia, take her and pour her over herself as if she were water. She places her fingers on her forehead and closes her eyes; she feels like she is drawing youth from her skin, desire tightens her throat.

"Two years ago, in Venice, I sold the Tintoretto house," says Irene. "You know, of all the real estate markets, Venice is the most interesting. Since the announcement at the COP34 in Nusantara that by 2042 the city will be submerged by the sea, the value of real estate has skyrocketed. Doing business in Venice became the dream of every real estate agent: the volume of international buyers increased fivefold. Once the regular sales were over, only people like me remained. We started hunting for bankruptcy sales, looking into the origins of estates and companies, rummaging through family affairs, spying. At a certain point, handling a property in Venice became so profitable that some of my colleagues, backed by the auction houses, thought they could enter the market by triggering the bankruptcy and failure of certain vulnerable businesses, of uninsured or precarious companies and estates ... but that's not the point. The reason why everyone wanted to buy a house in Venice is because by then it was assured that it would soon sink, and that, in twenty years, no building would be reachable. Investors were willing, and many still are, to pay millions to guarantee full ownership of these properties.

"For a long time, I didn't question their reasons, or the broader significance of this trend. As I said, I too was part of it. I only handled one property in Venice, and I guess I can consider myself fortunate. I landed the auction assignment through the intercession of the Korean consul, after a long series of deals, favors and good turns. Tintoretto's house is located along the Fondamenta dei Mori. It was completed in the fifteenth century, and its owner today is a twenty-four-year-old Bangalorean, son of the founder of a multinational telecommunications company. A refined, courteous, cultured young man. During our meetings and then at the signing of the deeds, we spoke about his studies in Europe, and his passion for the Mannerists. A year after the sale, the buyer invited me for a visit. He told me that, during the preservation work, the workers had accidentally broken through the east wall of the main floor, revealing a hollow partition. In the empty space, which in the sixteenth century must have been used for storage, sketches for the paintings decorating the choir of the church of the Madonna dell'Orto had been found. The buyer had not had them authenticated, but he was certain that they were originals by Tintoretto, preparatory sketches for the paintings of Temperance, Justice and Fortitude. He had the works hung in the living room. I told him it must be exciting to be able to invite someone to dinner and display the presence of such precious originals. He told me that he spent little time in Venice, perhaps ten or fifteen days a year, and that he preferred to enjoy the viewing alone. He had invited me to thank me for the incredible gift that I had unknowingly given him. I think it was the first and only time I felt revulsion for my work. I even thought about reporting him, but then I refrained: the process would have been long and onerous, and I would have been on my own, dealing with a rather powerful potential enemy. The buyer knew that reporting him would have been out of the question for me, or he would never have invited me there to thank me. He wanted to grant me the privilege of a look as a show of gratitude.

"I have often wondered whether he had not in fact approached the property already informed, or at least guided by a suspicion. Just as often I've wondered why I had never considered that prospect before the sale, and the answer is that it wasn't important to me. I wanted to earn as much as possible from that auction, it was all I could think of. In order to continue doing my job, I had to give up a certain kind of sensibility. Still, over the years, I have accumulated a considerable store of data, and this appreciable amount of information is unavoidably filed away in memory. Most of the sales I've handled in the last ten years have been of historic properties that, until a dramatic point in recent times, were considered public cultural patrimony: places to which anyone could have access. I've sold churches that have become wellness centers, buildings transformed into summer residences or offices, and the Tintoretto house was but one point in a long sequence of more or less advantageous negotiations. Those who came after me were denied the enjoyment of a certain vista, of a particular work of art, of a specific fresco or sculpture, and the thought of having been the last to set eyes on such beauty and right afterwards the last to cause my fellow man to be deprived of that beauty ... Even though I was aware of having certainly played a marginal role in the process of destruction which is of a much greater magnitude, even knowing that someone else would have taken my place if I had stepped aside ... in spite of that ..."

"It's not your fault," Lidia stops her. "The process you're talking about began before you were born."

"Collective guilt is nothing more than the sum of individual acts," Irene says.

"Why do they buy houses in a place that is about to disappear?" the girl asks, after a few moments of silence.

"The desire to possess is greater than fear, and in fact, many of them are convinced that owning will save them from disaster. At the same time, they are so wealthy that, even fully aware, they can afford to invest in properties that will not survive the next fifteen years. It's a muscular demonstration of power."

Lidia doesn't reply, as if she has already seen the story's conclusion coming: a huge approaching force, unstoppable.

Irene imagines her gratitude long before it has a reason to exist, and projects onto the girl's face the reaction to the words she is about to say. A profound sense of well-being fills her.

"I can't sell this house," she says. "Not now that I know what it means to you."

Lidia stares at her, motionless, her head still resting

on her lap, then she grips her wrist, forcing Irene to lean over her.

“Again. Say it again.”

“I can’t sell this house, now that I know what it means to you.”

The girl lets her go and closes her eyes. For a long moment she lies still in that pose of peaceful bliss, and seems to be savoring the meaning of every syllable.

“I can’t sell this house,” she repeats once more.

Before Irene can move, Lidia props herself up and burrows her face against Irene’s breast. With a hand she lifts the edge of her shirt, exposing the rosy areola.

For a long moment, Lidia slowly rubs her face, forehead, lips, and cheeks on Irene’s skin, until Irene pulls her close, pressing a hand on her head. The girl responds by sliding her mouth to the nipple; taking it between her lips she begins to suck gently, looking at Irene. She sucks innocently, under Irene’s petrified gaze, until she’s satisfied, then remains still with her face on her breast. As if she had performed the most natural act in the world, she falls asleep there.

1985

Lidia observes the hollow interior of the circular walls; this week they began laying the glass blocks. Dario tries never to lose sight of her when they are together on the building site, careful to pick up the slightest sign of dissatisfaction. For a few weeks, he has wondered about the possibility of having misinterpreted her. Perhaps displays of disappointment in Lidia are atypical, unrecognizable, like many other things about her. Yet she seems to answer every direct question sincerely and Dario has no choice but to believe her.

"I think I can see it," says Lidia, her gaze still turned upwards.

"What?"

"The house, once it's finished. It all seems clear to me."

"You think so?"

"Yes, it's very similar to what I imagined from the plan. So similar that it almost surprises me. When reality is too close to what is imagined I never know how I should feel."

"You'll like it."

"I have no doubt," says Lidia. "I won't be going on vacation this year," she adds. "My mother is leaving next week. We have a house in Romazzino."

"The city is desolate in the summer. You should go with her."

“But I can’t go. I’m a prisoner. Everything I care about is happening here.”

Lidia opens her arms to him. When Dario holds her, he is struck by a gesture he had only seen his son do, a year or two before: Lidia’s left hand clenched and then opened twice.

“Where will you go this summer?”

At the end of June, after a long discussion, Carla leaves for Genoa with the children. Upon her arrival, she calls as promised. She repeats that she is happy to be with her parents, but not about going there alone while he is staying in the city to work. The sun is beautiful, she says.

In Milan as well, for a few weeks, the state of grace persists. The neighborhoods begin to empty in the second half of July. At Via Saterna there is the smell of whitewash and sand. In the early afternoon the workers take a break, and Dario and Lidia with them. They walk to her mother’s house, not far from Via Saterna. They stroll in the sunlight like acquaintances, talking only about construction and nothing else, until the moment they get to Lidia’s room and close the door behind them. When it’s very hot, the cleaning lady opens the Venetian blinds halfway and screens the light with white curtains. In Lidia’s room there is a large portrait of her father, seated at his desk; when they are together, she never looks at it. On those afternoon breaks, Lidia perspires. The sweat creates a film on the skin between her shoulder blades and on her back, and forms tiny bubbles between her breasts, like the scales of a sea creature. She is on top of him, her cheeks and mouth flushed from the heat.

They spend the rest of their time at the construction site, both of them overseeing the work until evening, or rather Dario oversees it and Lidia, right behind him, registers his exchanges with the foreman, his exasperation, his insistent questions. She drifts off into the garden when the confrontation takes on more heated tones. From a distance Dario feels her watching him as she rests her ankles in the grass, and he pretends to lose his temper.

When evening comes, they often make the trip back together. Each day Dario finds himself deliberating on the wealth of Lidia's family, of Lidia herself as the sole heir now that her father is gone; since the day the demolition began, she has no longer spoken of his death. Before going to sleep or going out, Lidia shakes the dust from her hair in the bathroom. Dario imprints the memory of her naked body in his mind, the dark mass of hair and white particles that for a moment swirl around her, as if she had been pulled from an excavation. They fall into the habit of sleeping together, which at once seems risky to him. In the morning, they stay in bed till late, discussing the progress of the construction. It is always at that moment that Dario makes his requests, if he needs to: the expansion of this or that detail of the original plan, the selection of a more costly material, the proposal of a more modern solution. Potential improvements come to him during sleep. He often dreams of his doppelganger walking through the already completed construction, of finding himself far removed in time, surveying the particulars with a future eye and a clear mind. When he wakes up, his most pressing desire is to implement that whole series of small revelations that had appeared along the way. Lidia never objects: she listens to his explanations in silence, says yes; later in the day, when he thinks she has forgotten about their conversation, she hands him an envelope with a check.

They spend the weeks in symbiosis. For most of the time they are together, Lidia is serene. Often, however, she is absent, even when she is there. During a discussion, her eyes wander around or focus elsewhere. One night, Dario catches her standing motionless in front of her father's portrait. Her back is turned to him, her hands clasped around her throat. The following day, he pretends he didn't see it. Lidia's devotion to him, to the project ... Dario suddenly thinks he's happy.

Three days after her last encounter with Lidia, Irene uploads the online presentation information for Via Saterna. The latest news banner scrolls along the search engine's dashboard: another huge fire has broken out in Sasbachwalden, in the Black Forest. The news is accompanied by an aerial shot of the Mummelsee: the soaring temperatures have caused the lake to dry up.

On Monday, at Via Saterna, she and Lidia fill the pool with water. The play of reflections works even without the sun's participation, thanks to a system of lamps distributed along the hollow walls of the staircase. Irene imagines that, like herself after the projection of the 1980s originals, Lidia too is no longer satisfied to settle for artificial lighting. All the same, both compromise and give in to the allure of simulation, and in the evening, with the rest of the house in darkness, they linger to watch the enormous moving friezes of light on the walls. When the display slows down, Lidia reaches out a finger and replays the scrolling images, repeating a gesture that seems ingrained, a childhood memory.

In the final days, before everything starts shifting again, they spend their time around the pool as if sitting around a fire. Irene senses its significance, what the house might mean for Lidia, what it must have meant for the person who built it, and for the one who must have been the first to see it, namely the girl who died there. The circular, magnetic flow of affections, entanglements, memories, the designer's choice to place, at its center, a series of hypnotic distractions. Looking at the watery reflections, Irene seems to plunge backwards, in a spiral whose absence of meaning is salvific.

Just as often, Irene develops a deep sense of foreboding simply by looking at the pool. It feels as if danger were flowing underground, and that the water were reflecting its gaze, like on the day she discovered Lidia's portrait. Some evenings, the whole house seems to be watching. Or perhaps it is the solitude, Irene's sensation of being able to observe herself and Lidia from a vast distance, two illuminated points in an eternal void. By chance or by instinct, Lidia often interrupts her reflections before they drag her elsewhere. She persuades Irene to go out, to venture farther past the border.

One afternoon, they come to Torre Velasca. Lidia explains to her that the tower is patrolled by the police, and that in any case, the building's apartments, shops and offices are now almost all abandoned, with the exception of some surviving businesses on the ground floor. One of those that has persisted is an electronics parts store. Lidia leads her on a tour of aisles crammed with battery chargers. Under the watchful eye of the Indonesian clerk, she handles all the items, moving many into the wrong compartments. In a low voice, she tells Irene that, two years ago, the owner refused to hire her, and since then, she has periodically returned to create disorder. Leaving the store, Lidia guides her to the elevator.

"I've seen some vintage photos of this building," the girl says, looking at the scratches engraved on the mirror. "It was very beautiful. It's my favorite on this side of the city. All the places I like the most are the ones that were beautiful before I was born. I feel like I can't relate to anything that wasn't beautiful in the days before mine. I feel like I can only fall in love with abandoned, grungy, dilapidated places, because I'm certain they were once majestic. For example, from photos and videos you can see that at one time the lights here were warm. The blue neon was installed five years ago, after the building was stormed during a blackout. After that happened, the last decent tenants moved out and the military arrived. But you know these things better than I do, right?"

"Is anyone free to enter now?" Irene asks.

"Sure," Lidia replies, grabbing the handle of the glass door at the end of the corridor. "Just as long as they don't do anything foolish." The girl points to the ceiling, to show Irene the black eye of a camera. "Anyway, no one dangerous would come in here. Too many cops. Besides, there's nothing left to steal or to see ... except for this."

The draft of air sucks in the sharp, dry smell of the wind, the current ruffling their hair. On the terrace, however, the air is still. Lidia approaches the parapet; ahead of her is the view. The landscape, or what remains of it, spreads out before her. The city lies below, obscured by patches of fog drifting lower down, forming a thick blanket as it rises, creating a ceiling over their heads.

"I always come here when I'm scared," Lidia says, looking down.

From the ground come intermittent flashes of an inverted storm. The city sprawls out in a reverberation of artificial lighting, multiplied in capacity and range: a spectacle, Irene thinks, that only twenty years ago would have been impossible for her to conceive.

"That's where the camps begin," Lidia says, pointing to the southeast. "It's best not go to where there's no electricity."

The darkness extends chaotically, spreading out in a spiral. Lidia relaxes her shoulders and opens her arms, tilting her head back. For a moment, Irene has a twinge of apprehension, and reaches out to the railing. The girl simply takes a deep breath, then goes on gazing, expressionless, at the gray expanse of the landscape.

"This is where I come," she says. "It's happened to me often in the last five years. Feeling hopeless. When I remember that there is no hope, I come here. Everything is sliding towards the precipice, I feel drawn against my will; the mechanism that will soon annihilate me was set off a long time ago, before I was born. I come here when the thought of destruction scares me, and I wish I could to go back to a time I never knew, when someone could have reassured me. All I have to do is look down. I'm sure that if you think about it for a moment, you'll understand me. Is knowing that something else will survive us really the worst that can happen? Is being forgotten really the worst thing? And even if the end is irreversible this time, what difference does it make? Reminding myself that I am destined to vanish gives me a profound sense of well-being, like a video of the sea when it's calm. I'm just like that: solitary and at peace."

Irene listens and, although the exact meaning of Lidia's words escapes her, she seems to grasp their deeper essence, not the phrases themselves but their significance, distilled into a sensation: the resolution of the void between the body and the rest of the world.

Lidia goes to her and hugs her, resting her head between her neck and shoulder. Irene feels Lidia's eyes opening and closing, the brush of her lashes on her skin. It seems as though she has come a long way, and that for the first time in many years, she is aware of what is around her. The radical change that she wanted to ignore, taking refuge elsewhere, the energy spent in denial and in her work, she along with her acquaintances, her friends, hiding behind their professional dedication, in rebuilt ruins in the outskirts, in houses in gated communities, the universe beyond their generation and their social class a confusion of data unworthy of reflection and interpretation, or else overinterpreted and discussed until they've been drained of meaning.

With Lidia close to her, Irene seems to see the world again for what it has become, for what it is becoming, so different from what it was twenty years ago, from memories dragged forward, dwelled on beyond the limit of tolerance.

During the two weeks in which the sale of Via Saterna is open to bids, Irene sets the date for her appointment at the Adora clinic, buys Lidia some clothes, works on the documents under Ferrari's supervision.

Irene's father is confined to bed due to the sudden worsening of his illness. Her mother takes care of him and confides to Irene that lately these crises come and go often. She doesn't add anything else, and their conversations always end in respectful silence. During those two weeks, Irene almost never leaves Via Saterna. Although she worries about the risk of a surprise visit from Ferrari, even if he never comes, she stays with Lidia, constantly ready to warn her to hide. Though with each passing day Lidia's mood swings from forlorn to euphoric, often to despair, she never complains.

The night before the auction, Irene feels as though the entire time spent in the house, since she first set foot in it for the inspection, has been one extremely long, exhausting, horrific day. The definitions of temporal limits dissolve, and when she sees Lidia asleep beside her on the sofa, it seems as if she is seeing the girl for the first time, identical to how she looked the first time. She feels light, as if someone else were looking after her.

In a lingering, troubled sleep, worn out by her own lies, Irene has a kind of vision, a dream, in which Lidia weeps with gratitude, with joy. Every detail of her face is clear, down to the most minute detail: the creases, the skin gliding over the muscles, the color of her eyes, black. Within the pupil, a great blaze glows, ever closer.

1985

On the day the demolition of the old building on Via Saterna is completed, Dario takes his children to school. For a long time afterwards on the subway, he is bothered by the afterimage of their white smocks wrinkling as they slowly get out of the car and walk from the parking lot to the gate. Carla would say that it's another of his *hyperfixations*. That's what she's called them since he spoke to her about them a few years ago: the unpredictable shapes that his eye registers and retains on his retina, as if stuck on with glue. It happened again, more intensely than ever before, after his last meeting with Lidia.

He has never abided by the amorous flings and justifications of friends with lovers. He has always been repelled by the accounts and even confessions, finding them disturbing. Thinking about himself, seeing himself projected onto that model, makes him feel debased. The only explanation he can accept is the one that seems most natural: Lidia was inevitable, he never had time to avert the situation. It was meant to be that way, and so it was.

On Via Saterna, the walls have been knocked down. In the south wing of the house there's an opening from which you can see the sky. The interior layout had had to be completely demolished: only the load-bearing structures survived, the skeleton of the three floors, which could not be destroyed without risking collapse.

The living room where he first met Lidia is now a pile of rubble. At the thought of her, he sees her, as if she had materialized prompted by memory. She is standing in front of him, in the center of the exploded space of the room.

"Good morning," she says, smiling at him.

Dario looks at her shoes, the sandals with the blue heels, her bright-green dress. In the midst of the destruction she seems impeccably pristine.

"Good morning. What are you doing here?"

"I wanted to see."

"It's not safe, you could hurt yourself."

"I can watch my step," she says, moving carefully through the rubble. "We need to talk."

"Not here." Dario offers her a hand. "Let's go outside."

In the garden, Lidia wraps her arms around her waist. She is holding a set of keys, as if she left the house in a hurry.

"When does construction start?"

"As soon as the demolition is finished ..."

"And when will that be?"

"Next week at the latest."

"Good. I'm sure there's still time, and even if there isn't, I hope you'll forgive me."

Walking along the building's shattered perimeter, Lidia says, "I thought about it all night, I couldn't sleep a wink. I thought about the project, the plans you showed me, but above all, I hope you won't misunderstand me, not that the design on paper wasn't convincing, but I thought about what you said, and it was that, you see, more than any other objective evaluation. It's as if what you said and your voice, from that moment on ... What you said is true: the house isn't just ours; the house also belongs to those around us and those who will never be able to see the inside. The house embodies everything that surrounds it. I would like it if, in eighty or ninety years, when I'm no longer here, this house still had meaning," says Lidia. "I want it to have a significance apart from me, and I would like it to be built as if I didn't own it. I believe in your original plan, that's what I want."

"Then you'll have to talk to your fiancé again, don't you think?" Dario suggests.

"The plan he chose isn't the one I chose."

"But the house is yours and his."

"It's ours and it's my house too, my father left it to me before he died. It's my house." Lidia smiles. "This may be the first time in my life that I can exercise the right to have the final word. I want you to proceed with the original plan. I don't want a house for a family, I want the house you saw when you met me."

Dario nods. They go on walking in silence, covering the entire perimeter of the garden, until they're back to where they started.

"We'll have to tear something else out," Dario says, cautiously.

"Go ahead, I trust you."

Lidia looks at him, happy and defenseless; suddenly her inability to protect herself leaves him stunned. She has never been disappointed by anything, even her father passed away when he was still unmatched. The only grief she carries is inside, you can see it clearly, protracted as if cast by the setting sun. Dario wonders how she would respond to an inflicted pain, to a cruelty, since she seems so unprepared to see the risk.

"Can I come by later, when they've finished here?" she asks in a low voice, smoothing her hair back behind her ear with her fingers.

"Sure," Dario says, without thinking. "How tall are you, exactly?"

"Five foot five," says Lidia.

On the morning of the auction, Irene's father seems to have regained some of his strength: sitting in a nest of cushions propped up by her mother, he watches her guardedly as she enters the bedroom with an herbal tea in her hand.

"Are you in a rush?" he asks when Irene sets the cup on the nightstand.

She sits down at the foot of the bed, her leather jacket squeaking. She's spent a sleepless night, tense about the upcoming series of events. "No," she replies, unzipping the jacket.

Her father nods, pretends not to have noticed that she's about to leave, or maybe he really doesn't notice at all. That doubt has haunted Irene since her teenage years: what he really sees is the unsolved mystery of her and her siblings' defiance.

"How are things?"

"Good," Irene replies. "And you?"

"I've been bored to death lately." He ventures a provocative little smile. "Where do you have to go?"

"I have a couple of things to take care of for the auction."

"You're obsessed with work."

"I wouldn't say so."

"Of course you are. You take after me. You're the one who is most like me, out of all three of you."

"Ettore spends six months a year in Antarctica, for work."

"He does it for the money."

"So do I."

"No you don't."

Her father wins the set, Irene swallows it in silence. Looking at him in the morning light, or what's left of it, she is faced with the evidence of the sickly skin the color of dust, the wrinkles carved on a parched expanse.

"Don't think I've forgotten about it," her father says.

"About what?"

"The house. You have to take me there."

"I remember."

"Sunday, then. When your mother leaves for church."

Irene thinks about how her plan will have turned out by then. By Sunday everything will have already happened, something new will have already been set in motion. Should she ask Lidia to hide? Would her father understand? The crazy thought crosses her mind that he would understand immediately; maybe it is the simple hope of believing that he has changed, now that he seems so close.

Irene's cell phone rings. She lets it ring, doesn't move even as her father looks at her questioningly.

"Sunday," she says, when the ringing stops.

Her father nods, and leans his head back on the large pillow covered in blue silk. "I'll be ready."

For a moment, as Irene says goodbye to him, she imagines bending down and kissing him on the forehead, then resists the idea of a reaction that neither of them would understand. She settles for straightening the collar of his pajamas.

Leaving the room, she zips up her jacket again and proceeds unhurriedly down the stairs to the garage. She takes her cell phone out of her pocket when she is on the motorbike. Ferrari's number lights up at the top of the notification list. She makes the call as the gate slides closed horizontally.

"Sorry, I didn't pick up in time."

"Ms. Sartori," the lawyer says, his voice leaden. "Would you meet me in my office? As soon as possible."

The attorney is in his office, sitting in a rust-colored armchair. He is staring at the top of the cane gripped firmly in his hands and held out in front of his crossed legs, as if he were about to stand up. A potential move he's been about to make for at least ten minutes.

"I don't understand how that's possible," says Irene, running a hand through her hair. "I can't understand, everything was perfect," she adds. "I told you, I did what I always do, I considered everything down to the most minute detail, I did my research."

Ferrari has been listening to her apologies for half an hour. He's not furious, he looks at her with a trace of listless pity, as if she hadn't been invited but had shown up at his door as an unwelcome guest.

"It was all taken into account. Do you understand what I mean?" says Irene.

"No, I don't understand," says Ferrari, coldly. "You had a job and failed, which means I had a job and failed. The creditors will be furious. When I tell them the auction had no bidders, they will think I chose the wrong professional and that therefore I have become senile."

"Believe me, no one could have done a better job than me."

"Fine, I believe you," the lawyer says resignedly, exhausted. "But now be quiet for a minute, please."

Irene obeys, and for a long moment the man closes his eyes and rubs his index finger along the furrows on his forehead. When he opens his eyes again, he stares at her with compassion again.

"I firmly believed that the only person capable of selling that house was you. I still believe it. I also believe that, if you were not able to do it, it is because the property is unsellable."

Ferrari stands up quickly, which Irene thinks she's only seen him do on the last visit to Via Saterna. He leans on the desk, looks around in vain for something, perhaps a drink, a bottle that ran out who knows when and was never replaced.

"In any case—" Ferrari says.

"Maybe it was the news of the fire," Irene interrupts him. "The markets always get unnerved when natural disasters are around."

"The Black Forest, you mean?" Ferrari asks, laconically.

"That's right. It's spreading on all fronts at an unprecedented speed."

"Of course, I understand, listen ..."

"But what happens now? What will happen to the house?" Irene asks.

The lawyer gives her an apathetic look. Having finished explaining the disaster, it must seem like a waste of time to devote his attention to someone who can't solve his most pressing problem. He stands stiffly, waiting for the right moment to dismiss her.

"Nothing will happen. I haven't had any success with private individuals. I'll have to turn to the state,"

Ferrari replies. “They pay very little but the creditors are bloodthirsty: if they can’t have the sale itself, they will settle for the *idea* of the sale.”

“But it would be a huge waste, it’s a fantastic property.”

Ferrari erupts in a bitter laugh. “Dear God, *a fantastic property*. So *fantastic* that in the end no one wanted it.”

“It’s just an unfortunate time, I’m sure that at the right moment—”

“Ms. Sartori, there will never be a right moment. We haven’t experienced a right moment for at least thirty years.” Ferrari presses the cane into the palm of his pale hand. “I had warned you: this house is ill-fated. Believe me, I’m not surprised.”

“Why do you say that?”

“Because right now I should be in my own house, in the countryside, far from Milan, and instead I’m here. This house has kept me tied up here for longer than I had planned, much longer. I’ve exhausted my patience with this house, and to be totally honest, I hate it, I despise it. Nothing good could come of it.”

Irene looks away. “What if I told you I have a buyer?”

Ferrari is impassive, but she can already see the calculation that her unexpected question has triggered, the mental collection of risk factors. “Listen, I can find you a buyer, I’m serious. I already have someone in mind.”

The last assertion doesn’t seem to sway Ferrari; on the contrary, it seems to irritate him.

“You just have to give me time to contact him and put out a feeler. I could come back to you with an offer this very evening. This is an investor I’m already familiar with, I know his tastes, his assets. At least let me try. What do we have to lose?"

Ferrari studies her as if he were assessing a contract or an agreement between the parties.

"You know the state would pay very little. I am certain my buyer's offer would be higher. Would the creditors care if the auction period were extended until tomorrow, or later?"

"Not at all," the attorney replies. "The creditors have blind faith in my abilities. They have worked with me all their lives; their fathers worked with me before they were born."

"Good. Let me negotiate with my contact. If the deal closes, and I am sure it will, tell the creditors that there was only one buyer at the auction, willing to make just one final offer, and that you thought it was expedient to conclude the sale. You must have already predicted that it was a high-risk property, you're too experienced not to have anticipated the situation. The creditors are already aware that you considered the operation a hopeless endeavor."

"Sartori, stop," Ferrari grumbles. "You make me feel young again when you say that."

Irene suppresses a victorious smile. She tears a piece of paper from the Via Saterna plan, picks up a pen from the table, and writes down a figure. She then hands the note to the attorney.

"I think I can negotiate for this number."

Ferrari leans forward politely, calculates, and remains still for a very long moment. Slowly, he lets himself break into a full smile. When he smiles, exposing ivory-colored teeth and bluish gums, Irene suddenly sees him as an exhausted man.

"Do you think you can resolve it with a phone call?" he asks.

"Send me the contract and give me until tomorrow morning. I'll be in touch as soon as I have an answer."

Ferrari calls up the contract file on his laptop, and sends her the document. When Irene leaves his office, he falls into a lengthy silence.

1985

"I'll give you a copy of the keys," Lidia says when they meet at the gate.

Once they enter, she goes off to the dining room and leaves him alone in the living room to sort out the plans. Dario hears her walking about in the next room, then the sound of her footsteps gradually fades as she moves away, opens the windows at the back, in the kitchen. Many of the load-bearing walls are not indicated on the plan of the old house. Back in the living room, Lidia unlocks the French window. Out of the corner of his eye, he sees her step out into the garden. He hears her return after a brief look around; the sound of her footsteps annoys him. She dawdles along until she joins him.

"What is it?" she asks.

"The plan," Dario replies, not taking his eyes off the blueprint. "I'm trying to figure out if we can knock down a wall or if we have to keep it."

"Which one?"

"That one," he points in front of them.

Cartons and books have accumulated in the house, which has evidently been abandoned for a long time. A barrier of stuff is stacked up to the ceiling, covering the wall. Moving around the sofa, Dario unbuttons his shirt cuffs, rolls the sleeves up to his elbows, and begins to dismantle the barricade from the top. He grabs a box and, as soon as he shifts it, hears the sound of broken porcelain.

"They'll come to empty everything out in a few days," she says, behind him.

"No problem."

"I'll help you."

"No, there's no need."

"I have nothing to do."

Lidia staggers for a moment under the weight of a large carton, then, at the last moment, regains her balance.

"Please don't hurt yourself," Dario begs her, watching her move precariously on her heels.

"I won't hurt myself."

Together they slide the boxes toward the entrance. The heaviest ones, at the base of the pile, contain enormous encyclopedic volumes. It takes two to move them far enough away to clear access to the wall. They finish the job without speaking, and Dario climbs over an old gramophone and stares at the wall, studying it; with a rap of the knuckles, it rings hollow.

"Perfect, just as I thought."

"What?"

"We can remove it."

"Good," Lidia breathes a sigh of relief, wiping her face with a hand.

They are both sweaty and heated; Dario immediately feels embarrassed. She turns around and disappears through the kitchen door. "It's terribly hot," she grumbles. "I forgot they turned the water off in here." He follows her in search of air: when he looks into the room, he sees her lying on the ground, on the terracotta floor.

"It's nice and cool here, try it."

Dario stares down at her, suddenly feeling out of place, his presence inappropriate.

"If you don't do what I say I'll feel stupid," Lidia insists.

He imitates her, settling down beside her at a distance he considers proper. Lying on his back he can instantly feel the cool tiles through his shirt, then through his hair, on the nape of his neck, through the thin layer of his pants. Instinctively he spreads his hands palm down: the coolness seeps through them too, numbing him.

"This was my grandmother's house," says Lidia. "It has always been very hot. I don't remember much about the last years, but sometimes in May my parents would go away for the weekend and leave me here. I spent every afternoon lying on the floor, often under the table. It was the only place she hadn't covered with carpets. I've never liked this house, I'm glad it's about to be torn down."

She stares at the ceiling while she speaks, as if she's forgotten that he's lying there next to her. By now Dario is too exhausted to notice any absurdity in the situation. It's as if all the fatigue accumulated in the past few months—the job that never materialized, the job that in the end did turn up, the meeting with the future spouses, the threat of being fired—had crashed down on him the moment he gave in to Lidia's urging. He remains still under a world that has given way. When he hears the girl sobbing, he thinks he himself has started crying without realizing it; he touches his nose, his cheeks, certain they will feel wet, but instead they are dry, and it's Lidia who is crying. He sees her wipe her eyes, hears her sob again.

"What's wrong?" he asks, not moving.

"It's nothing, I'm sorry," Lidia shakes her head. "I apologize. You must think I'm crazy, but I'm not, I'm just tired."

"A few months ago my father died," she continues. "He had been ill for a long time, but I didn't understand what it really meant, until the time came. I always felt that my life was moving very slowly, but for six months now it seems to have started speeding along twice as fast. Since his death my life has done nothing but race ahead of me and I can't stop it—it speeds on, presses forward, runs ahead without me. It seems to me that my whole existence is nothing but a dark line moving forward, the same things continue to repeat themselves, but faced with these things I am older every day, and also more weary, and all these things continue to flow past those that came earlier, they surpass the memory that preceded them, as if from this moment on I could not escape, not even if I wanted to, so that the future appears to be a bottomless nightmare, it's as if I could see it: today everything I love is gone, consumed, I no longer recognize anything that is around me, I am no longer me but a body that moves about dispersed in an eternal fog. And so all the promises that are made to me today, the promises that I also made to myself, of a bright, radiant future, already seem broken."

Dario listens to Lidia, this very young woman, speak as if extracting the words from her head. Or maybe he only imagines that's what she's saying, maybe she said something completely different but he will only be able to remember it the way he imagined it.

Lidia takes a deep breath, then turns her head to look at him.

"The first design you showed us was magnificent. I had no idea that a house could be so majestic, nor that it could so little resemble the houses I have always seen. You designed a grand, striking house. You deserve to build it," she says in a rush. "I no longer know if I want to get married."

Very early the following morning, Irene calls Ferrari. "Sartori, don't tell me," he answers quickly, as if he had been waiting for her phone call all night.

"I've sent you a copy of the contract signed by the buyer," she says. "For fiscal reasons, he prefers to proceed with the purchase through his company. I don't believe that's a problem for you."

Ferrari reads the name Audax from the contract.

"It's a Meta company," Irene explains. "Don't ask me for more. If you want I'll have the buyer contact you."

"I don't think that's necessary."

Ferrari is silent, a faint crackle comes from the phone.

Irene pictures him bending over the computer screen, scrolling through each page.

"I asked the buyer to proceed with full payment immediately. He used the coordinates in the contract, you should receive a deposit in the next forty-eight hours. I've attached a receipt," Irene adds.

"Ms. Sartori ..." The man's voice fades off, he's smiling.

"I told you I would sell it."

"Yes, you said so," Ferrari says. "I'll see the notary this very day to deliver the documents."

"But it's Saturday. Is the notary available?"

"He will be for me," Ferrari's voice smiles again. "Congratulations, Ms. Sartori."

*

When Irene gets to Via Saterna, Lidia isn't there. She searches the house, the green room, and finds her few belongings there: two pairs of pants folded in the closet, the gray sweatshirt—she must be wearing her only pair of shoes, and the shoulder bag has also accompanied her on her outing. That's how Irene imagines her, on a brief break to distract her from the idea of her lost home.

Irene knows that Lidia will return, she always returns, unable to get over the prospect of abandonment. For a while, she sits on the bed, dressed, then gives in to weariness. She takes off her jacket, her boots, her T-shirt, and drops back on the covers, feeling peacefully exhausted, as if she had reached her destination at the end of a long journey. She slips off her pants and panties together, unhooks her bra, kicks her clothes to the floor. She slides toward the pillow, lifts up the sheets, and pulls them close around her. Lying on her back, she's thinking and at the same time not thinking.

The bed has been slept in by others before her, before Lidia, perhaps it's suggestivity or the bliss she seems to have been preparing for during the last three long weeks, but the only thought she feels emanating from things is love. In other houses she's felt watched, but never with this gaze, intense and benevolent, that radiates like a caress from the ceiling and from the corners of the room.

Irene shifts onto her stomach under the sheets, her cheek sinking into the pillow where Lidia breathes. In the silence of the house, when she is about to give in to sleep, she becomes aware of the weight of another body on hers; from the force that embraces her, heat spreads from head to head and then inside her. Irene feels as though she is crying: it happens at a moment which she is no longer able to remember.

The sound of the front door, two floors below, wakes her up: it opens, then closes. Irene sits up, drags her legs off the bed; with her heart still asleep, she quickly puts on her clothes, struggles with the zipper of her boots. Even on her feet she feels drained. Drifting off into a deep sleep had projected her into the darkness of evening. She gropes her way down the corridor, to the stairs. On the ground floor the only thing visible are the cones of light cast by the lamps suspended over the dining table. In the shadows, Irene sees Lidia walk quickly to the nearest switch; an instant later, Via Saterna is brightly lit.

Lidia looks up at her.

"You scared me."

Irene goes down the stairs, careful where she steps: her muscles are shaking, hesitant. Lidia is sitting on the sofa. From up close she looks rumpled, her eyes are red, her hair tangled. She stares at her.

"Well?" she asks.

"The house is sold," Irene replies.

The girl nods. "Of course, I thought so. But how much time do I have? When will the owners arrive?"

Lidia seems to be holding her breath. For a moment, Irene is able to grasp the thought of having lost everything. She imagines being able to feel the despair of being alone in the world. She hesitates, prolongs the pleasure of her revelation.

"The owner is already here," says Irene.

"What do you mean?"

"The auction had no bidders," Irene replies. "I made sure it wouldn't."

"What are you saying?"

"I'm saying I had an idea," says Irene. "Not really an idea, more of a modification."

At the beginning of Irene's career, Paolo, who at the time was still her shadow, had taken her to a funeral. The deceased was one of the leading figures in the capital's real estate business. The first of the ventures to which he owed his fame, "more than to the ridiculous amount of money he had managed to make," as Paolo had explained to her, the deal for which everyone remembered him, was having caused the failure of a competitor's auction. Specifically, he had first made sure it had no bidders, and then he had come forward himself to acquire the property at a bargain price. He had succeeded by anonymously contacting those who had submitted purchase offers, and sending them a dossier that demonstrated the presence of a toxic waste landfill a few yards from the property in question: a farm in the Tuscia Viterbese region. The potential buyers had backed out, and he had submitted the only offer through a front man. When, several years later, suspicions of fraud arose, the property had already become one of the most profitable agritourism businesses in Lazio, and the bidder had committed suicide after a series of disastrous transactions. Everyone knew about it, many admired him. Though Paolo was appalled by it, he had nevertheless sent a wreath of white roses to the altar.

The idea of a bogus technical report therefore came from her previous life, and it was easy to find a plausible pretext: Irene chose the house's foundations. Milan's problem with the aquifer is no secret, the city's progressive sinking is known to all, and the incidents of recent years have been reported in the international news. Irene completed a report on how the structure of Via Saterna had been irreversibly compromised by variations in the height of the foundations. Putting together the documentation wasn't difficult; she included photos of damage found in other properties: bulging floors and ceilings, longitudinal cracks in load-bearing walls, and so on, and was careful to suggest credible perspectives and angles. She retrieved the contact details of potential buyers from the proposals to which both she and Ferrari have access, and, three days before the auction, she sent an email to all of them from an anonymous address.

Once this first phase was completed, she found the frontman: a virtual, anonymous company, started three or four years earlier when investing in the Metaverse was not yet prohibitive. She had concluded transactions with Audax only twice before, and this was the first involving such a high capital. By the time she has to declare the purchase under her real name for tax purposes, Ferrari will already be far away and no longer interested in Via Saterna.

"What matters is that the house is mine now," Irene concludes. "You don't have to leave. It was the only thing I could do. I didn't want you to lose the house, and I didn't want to lose it either, but I couldn't afford to compete with the offers. I had to rig the game, or we would both have lost. Look, I did all this because I want you to stay here, I don't want you to ever have to sleep in the train station again. I want to help you with your studies, help you finish university. You have to come and live here again, you have to leave all your things here, go back to living a normal life. Lidia, are you listening to me?"

Irene bends down to the girl sitting on the sofa, who is looking at her petrified. Instinctively, her hand reaches out to Lidia's hair, tries to smooth a few dusty strands. "See, I really love you, I don't want to abandon you, I want you to stay here with me. Do you understand me? I would like you to have a somewhat happy life again. I want to help you."

Lidia pushes her away. "I can't."

"Can't what?"

"I can't stay here with you."

Lidia takes Irene's face in her hands and draws her towards her; Irene leans forward, falls to her knees. The girl strokes her cheeks, rests her forehead on hers, she is so close now, Irene can't focus on her.

"I would really like to ..." she says in a low voice, wrapping her arms around Irene for a moment, exploring her body as if she were looking for something. "Really," she repeats.

Lidia leans back a little, takes Irene's face in her hands again; her hands are warm now.

"I would like to be part of this dream of yours, this kind of retro, slightly incestuous delirium in which I would play the role of the poor girl to be rescued. I understand your dream and I'm touched." Lidia kisses her nose, then studies her with eyes that Irene has never seen, as if they weren't hers. "Do you seriously think I could settle for living here with you? Irene, Irene ... you are so disconnected from reality, you smell good, you're beautiful, but ..."

Lidia brushes her face against Irene's, then kisses her, stands up and looks down at her, bringing her head close to her groin.

Irene is not sure what is happening: reality diverges so intensely from her anticipation that she feels as if she is watching a well-thought-out joke. She feels nothing, except confusion. Then Lidia grows sad, and Irene recognizes the fear inside her: it crawls to her throat, creeping up from her legs, which were the first to understand the words.

"Please, don't look at me like that," the girl says, grabbing her by the arms. "Get up. Stand up."

Irene obeys: on her feet she is taller than Lidia again, but it is not enough to make her feel confident.

"It's your parents' house", she says. "I thought you would want … that you wanted to stay here, at home …"

Lidia nods, starts to cry but in a way that is completely different from what Irene is used to: she cries like an adult, she doesn't look away, she runs a hand over her mouth.

"I don't understand what you're saying," Irene says. She moves closer to her, caresses her shoulder.

Lidia nods again; now she's smiling hopelessly.

"That's exactly what I said, right?" her voice cracks. "I've also thought about it during these months, you know? I've thought about it for so long, more than I should have. I thought about me and you, day and night, about me coming to live here, and waking up here, coming back here every day. About you not leaving. During these months I thought I saw what you saw. Some days I genuinely believed it, that's why it's all been that much more difficult, you see? It's so hard …"

Lidia wraps her arms around herself, shaken by a sob.

"You have great persuasive skills, Irene," Lidia says. "You're so good you don't even need to speak. People believe you, don't they? They always do what you want, don't they?" Lidia runs her hands through her hair. "Very soon, whatever I say will no longer have any significance to you, but I just want you to know, I want you to know ... that if I could have, if it had all been real, I would have stayed. If I had been the person you think I am, I would have chosen to stay. I would have stayed here, with you, and there would have been no other place in the world where I could be happy." Lidia turns around, and walks toward the pool, magnetized by her portrait. Irene follows her as if in a trance.

"What are you saying?" she asks. "What do you mean?"

The girl circles the pool, moving to a safe distance. "It means that none of it is real. You should open your eyes, Irene, look beyond me and this story. You're building a perfect world in one that's already going to pieces. How long do you think it will take? Do you think your family and your money can protect you for much longer? Your birthright has protected you for forty years, and yet it's coming, that time ... You know what I want? To get away from here. To save myself. To escape as far away as possible from here."

"I don't understand."

"I'm not who you think I am. I'm not the Kowalskis' daughter. They probably didn't have children, and in any case it's none of my business. I'm no one's daughter. I had never seen this house, until a few months ago. It was all an act."

Irene struggles to assign a meaning to what Lidia is saying, her words pour out in an avalanche, overwhelming her with all the possible translations.

"Lidia, what are you telling me ..." Irene goes to the girl, grips her wrist; she's alive, she exists, and she's trying to free herself.

"Let go of me."

"What are you saying? Why are you saying these things? Do you know what I went through to get this house? Do you know the risks I took?"

"You did what you were supposed to do. Exactly as the attorney predicted."

Lidia struggles to get out of her grasp; Irene is holding her by the arms.

"What does that mean? Say something. Tell me what you mean!"

"Let go of me."

"No, talk. Now."

"Get your hands off me."

"What the hell did you mean?"

Lidia's shove sends Irene sliding backwards, toward the pool, her center of gravity shifting without warning. She falls into the water, landing on her back, and hits her head against the metal edge. For a few seconds, the blow stuns her. She's aware of the sound of Lidia's footsteps, focuses on her moving shadow. When she manages to get to her feet, dripping wet, she can see her clearly at the door.

The girl turns around before leaving, her face twisted in an anguished grimace. "Forgive me, please."

"What does that mean?" Irene repeats, running her hands over her face.

"Ask the attorney."

*

When Irene climbs out of the pool it's the middle of the night; maybe it was already late when Lidia came back and then left. Despite swiping her finger across the cell phone screen several times, the numbers and hours form a fragmented pattern, until the battery runs out. For a long time, Irene feels like she's shuffling aimlessly, chilled by the wet clothes between her legs and on her back. At one point she thinks about putting on Lidia's dry clothes, but she doesn't move. She sits at the dining table, unable to think, until dawn's reddish glow rises from the garden.

The day's arrival activates the circuits, the blood starts pulsing in her throat again, and Irene makes her way to the motorbike parked in the courtyard. The sky is smudged with the colors of fire, recalling the news reports she's read online, warning that the wind will soon push the great fire south. When she reaches Ferrari's studio, the fog is tinged with orange. It is very early, maybe six o'clock. Irene is certain that Ferrari is expecting her. She pictures him in his studio, waiting. As on the first day, she presses the intercom and the door opens with a click. Walking up the stairs, Irene can't feel anything, except an incredulous curiosity, as if she were observing herself from a great distance, a stranger to herself.

The door on the third floor is open. Irene goes in and closes it behind her in the silence of the blue hall. A light from the room at the end of the corridor casts a golden triangle on the carpet. She proceeds toward the office where she and the lawyer met for the first time to discuss the house. He is sitting at the table with his back to the door. She goes in and sits in the chair where she recited the story of the anonymous buyer.

The attorney also seems exhausted. He gazes at her for a long time, without speaking, as if she were a landscape.

"I haven't slept a wink either, believe me," Ferrari says finally.

Irene presses her knees together; she can still feel the water's chill in her joints. The attorney reaches into the inside pocket of his jacket, takes out a silver lighter and a cigarette, one of the old-style kind, with a filter. Irene recognizes the engraving on the lighter. Ferrari displays it like a jewel between his fingers, as he waits for the flame to catch.

"I am truly sorry," the lawyer blows away the first drag, looks at her, then lowers his eyes to the desk. "I wanted to tell you that the dossiers were perfect, and that I really appreciated the intensity and passion of your words. Even though you constructed them to deceive me, I believe there was some truth in them, and for that as well I must apologize. I feel there was pure, sincere feeling in what you said. Falling in love with places follows the same rules as falling in love does between people. I can't determine to what extent buying a property for a third of its value must have seemed like an irresistible opportunity to you, but I don't think you did it for that reason alone."

"I didn't do it for that," Irene interrupts. "I did it for Lidia. I thought Lidia needed help."

"Do you think you were tempted by my age? Maybe for a moment you saw me and thought you were more intelligent, more savvy. Don't get me wrong, I was like that too, at your age. In all honesty, I think you are very capable and intelligent, all this has nothing to do with the skills of either of us ... Besides, when I started out, I had an advantage."

"I am prepared to relinquish the house."

Ferrari slowly shakes his head. He seems sincerely regretful.

"You can't back out of the contract, even if you signed it on behalf of a shell company. You signed it, the notary certified it, the funds were transferred, the house is owned by the Audax company. The house is yours. I'm afraid that this matter won't end there."

"What do you mean?"

"Everyone will have to know," Ferrari replies slowly. "Monsignor Vallini, other friends in the curia, the professionals with whom you've worked, the owners of the properties you've sold. It has to be that way, it can't be otherwise."

Irene absorbs the meaning of his words, the future into which they cast her. Since her last meeting with Lidia, the world has been upended in a parallel, unreal dimension, a nightmare in which she herself breathes and moves as the protagonist.

"You can't do this to me."

"Unfortunately, I must. I won't take you to court."

"Who is Lidia?" she asks.

Ferrari remains silent, ponders the ash on the tip of his cigarette, then reaches out and taps it into the ashtray.

"The Lidia you met is a very bright, very talented girl, who needed the money and the job I offered her. The real Lidia, whom you never met, was a girl I knew forty-five years ago, when she was still a child," the man pauses for a long time. "The real Lidia was the most precious thing I ever had, until someone took her away from me."

"Who is the girl I met on Via Saterna?"

"A very talented girl. An actress."

"An actress?"

"Yes, Ms. Sartori. An actress."

"An actress? I don't understand ..."

"You have to forgive me." Ferrari offers an embarrassed smile. "Look, for now, try, really make an effort not to judge what happened. As with all inexplicable events, this story follows a logical course. It does not escape the rules of reality: none of us can do that. A year ago, you and I met for the first time. The occasion was a charity evening in the capital, and you were sitting some distance away from me. I was visiting Rome on behalf of the creditors, and was invited to the event by my dear friend Vallini. As we chatted, you see, I told Vallini that I had a property on my hands that I wanted to get rid of. You were a stranger to me until Vallini began to tell me about your skills, your background, your origins, your birthplace, your surname. At that point my interest became a suspicion, and, subsequent to my research over the following days, my suspicion became a certainty. I don't believe in destiny, Sartori. I believe in circular motion. That day, with you there, came right at the end of my life. At the end of this circle is my death, we both know it, but I was granted a pardon: I was offered the chance to bring about closure. This explains the girl, the actress you call Lidia, as well as a whole series of other things, the auction, the buyers, the painting. But in particular the girl. I have continued my observations for a year, and in my own way I am happy and at the same time saddened by the result. You did exactly what I expected. Of course, as I told you, I started out with an advantage: you didn't know me, whereas I knew you. As I said, I investigated and did my research, but that wasn't all: you are very much like your father."

"What does my father have to do with it?"

Ferrari pushes his chair back with one foot, lets himself lean back at the head of the table with a sigh: "*For I, the Lord thy God, am a jealous God, visiting the sins of the fathers upon the children unto the third and fourth generation*," he recites.

Irene stands up, goes to the door; she needs air, she can't breathe. Though until this moment she has wanted to know the truth, now it seems to her that every additional word could only be senseless insanity.

"Wait, before you go." The attorney stops her. "Don't you want to know why I did all this to you?"

"I'm reporting you."

"Don't say that, Sartori, what evidence do you have? Allow me to dissuade you. Consider retiring, change professions, take some time for yourself." Ferrari looks up at her. "I've produced so much evidence that you would lose at any stage of litigation. You would only be forced to give me more money. Is that really what you want? To squander all your savings on a case you've already lost?"

"I don't know you, I don't know who you are. You're a psychopath."

"I'm completely normal, believe me," Ferrari says, shaking his head. "You see, in this whole story there's only one guilty party, and it's neither me nor you. We are both victims of the same agent, the individual who forty years ago destroyed my life. Your father. Your father came into my life, into our lives, mine and Lidia's, with the precise intention of wrecking it. Lidia did not survive that intention."

Irene thinks of Lidia, the Lidia she knew, lying on the grave of the girl who died on Via Saterna; the copies of the news in the newspaper, the photo, the surname, her father's age, the lawyer's age, nothing makes sense, and yet the common thread seems to emerge from the water like a dead body. It's not possible.

"Your father never spoke to you about Via Saterna, or am I wrong? No one, except me, knows who built that house. The renowned architect Sartori entered Via Saterna when he was still a nobody. That house, which should have been the home of our children, became a tomb. That house made your father rich and famous and buried an innocent creature. Afterwards, he took care to erase the traces." Ferrari drags himself to his feet one last time, and approaches her. "Your father dumped Lidia as soon as his youngest daughter was conceived, Ms. Sartori, but you couldn't have known that. You were simply here, forty-two years later, in a position guaranteed by the prosperity your father promised you: beautiful, confident, successful, perfect. How could I resist? I had waited forty years for the circle to close."

Irene avoids his eyes and, without a word, makes her way down the dark corridor. His last words reach her when she's at the front door. Her hands are shaking on the handle.

"Give your father Cesare Ferrari's regards."

1985

The clients are an engaged couple, soon-to-be newlyweds, very well-off, Saverio had said. They have a property in the center, in the Castello area: they want to demolish the old house and build a new one. They are well-heeled, Saverio reiterated, money is not an issue.

Dario has arranged the meeting for Tuesday morning, a day that seems auspicious to him: a Tuesday at the end of April that already feels like spring. The street number is 7 Via Saterna, and he walks there, measuring the distance from Piazza Castello, watching the school children circling around the base of the fountain. The air is fragrant, and from the Castle to his destination he feels like he is walking on air. It is unquestionably one of those rare, very rare days when he still thinks he can believe in something.

When he gets there, he throws open the unlocked gate and climbs the three steps to the front door. He knocks twice, loud and clear, and immediately hears the sound of footsteps on the other side. A distinguished man slightly younger than himself, with green eyes, opens the door and smiles pro forma.

"Good morning, I'm here to discuss the renovation," Dario says.

The man reaches out and shakes his hand, drawing him inside.

"Wonderful, we were expecting you. Follow me, let's introduce ourselves," the man steps aside. "Please, over that way, my fiancée is waiting for us in the garden."

Dario walks through the entrance hall and then a living room, from there the man leads him into the kitchen, and from the kitchen to the garden.

"So then, you must be the architect," the man says, approaching the girl who is waiting for them in the shade.

"Yes, I'm Sartori," he introduces himself, holding out his hand. "Dario Sartori."

"It's a pleasure. Cesare Ferrari," the man says, returning a hasty handshake. "And this is Lidia, my future bride."

Lidia shakes his hand. For the entire duration of the meeting, she barely speaks, but watches intently. To Dario it seems that no detail escapes the unspeakable weight of her large, dark eyes that pause on everything. They linger and gauge, they measure his words, even her body seems to be appraising him, and he finds himself wondering on what scale a stranger could ever weigh what he brings along with himself.

During the encounter, the future groom provides very detailed information about what he wants, the criteria for the house—he is passionate about interior design, he says—and Dario listens. He listens and yet the only piece of information he takes with him at the end of the meeting is the unknown woman: he is certain he has seen her before elsewhere. Sometimes the city is such a small world that it's scary, sometimes the world is immense yet seems tiny.

Back at the studio, he gets to work in a way that only happens when he is inspired, and this inspiration is a voice that dictates the direction, the design, the form, everything that will come from now on the voice will dictate, like a stranger's eyes measuring him from head to toe, the voice will dictate a house that will endure forever, that will be forever.

"Irene?" Her father's voice surprises her on her return, coming from the living room as she has one foot on the stairs. "Irene, is that you?"

Irene catches a glimpse of herself reflected in the frame of a family photo: her face is worn, her eyes swollen, her skin patchy. She's exhausted, she's had no sleep, going non-stop, for hours and hours, and no food. She pulls her hair behind her ears, and rubs her hands over her face. She breathes into the image of her mother and her siblings, of her young father, standing upright: she is just a little girl.

She joins him in the living room. He is waiting for her dressed to the nines, an elegant suit, fit for a party. Irene wonders how he managed to convince her mother to let him wear it; she can imagine the questions her mother must have asked that morning.

"You're late," he says.

"Huh?"

"We have to go see the house, did you forget?" he says, peeved.

For a moment, Irene feels the urge to scream, to yell, to smash something.

"It's impossible to breathe outside, Dad."

It's true. The air is orange, and it's hot out there. On the way home the flashing emergency signals were on: *Climate alert, stay indoors.*

"Tomorrow will be worse," he says. Irene can hear a shadow of desperation in his voice. "I don't know if I'll feel well tomorrow. You have to take me there today."

"It's just a house, Dad."

Despite the insanity that occurred in Ferrari's office, despite the fear, the trick, her career, Irene immediately feels cruel. She sees her career falling to pieces, and yet, she feels sorry for her father: he's defenseless. For the first time, she could deny him what he wants and he would have no other way to make it happen, he would just have to give it up forever.

"But you said you would take me there."

"I did."

Irene turns, leaves the room abruptly, makes it to the kitchen bathroom before the urge to throw up overtakes her. She vomits bile into the sink, as spasms ripple down her spine, tightening her neck. When she is sure the fit has passed, she rinses her mouth under the thin stream from the faucet.

When she returns to the living room, he is waiting for her, his face glum.

"You're right," Irene says, going to him; she offers him her hand, and he immediately clings to it, maybe fearing that she will change her mind. "Let's go."

Along the way, they encounter very few vehicles, and the unfailing LED *climate alert* signs affixed to the stoplights at the street corners. Via Saterna is very close to her parents' house, so close that Irene wonders how her father managed to stay there so long, all his life, whatever happened, however Lidia died. The air is red-tinged when they arrive.

Irene helps her father out of the car. He starts coughing as soon as they reach the driveway. She watches him stare up at the house, at the second-story window facing east, and for a moment she feels very heavy, like molten metal. She pulls him toward her, guiding the walker to the front door. He enters first, and Irene closes the door behind them.

Her father doesn't speak, doesn't move. She waits to see some sign on his face, but he holds back, he looks at things with infinite patience, with the calm of a millenary stone.

"Do you like it?" Irene hears herself ask, after several minutes of silence.

He nods.

Irene goes to the dining table, where Lidia left the projector. She turns it on, carrying it with her to the central pool. She hears her father approaching from behind—his legs drag along with the creaking of the metal casters.

The projection spreads out, still jumbled at first, and then more stable, aligned, defined. He moves his head around—he feels it, but doesn't have the courage to look at it. When each level gains its proper position, the reflections of water and light return. Her father conceived the space, the reverberation of light, his mind willed it to be. The thought leaves Irene transfixed.

"It can get bigger, right?" he asks.

"Yes."

"Show me the second floor, the stairs."

Irene adjusts the projection, and the zoom lens brings the image of the second floor in front of them, the liquid shapes of the glass blocks distinguishable on the wall.

"To the right," says her father. "Even bigger."

Irene follows his instructions, until the search pays off: a detail that only the person who filmed the tape can know, a spot where neither she nor anyone else could have discerned a presence.

Behind the transparent stream of the corridor, where the inner circle of the stairs widens abruptly, stands a figure frozen in time. The glass distorts the female body, you can make out the bare arms, the white dress, the mass of dark hair, as if under an expanse of solid, undulating water. The facial features are motionless, caught in a recess, as are the eyes, eternally turned down, towards the photographer. Irene seems to sense love coming from that body trapped in the past, a shadow among the shadows that her father was looking for.

She holds her breath. This is the moment to talk, to confess and to ask for explanations, to tell him about the attorney, her wrecked career, to lay the blame on her father, the guilt that she can still only intuit. But the girl, the girl looks down below, into the depths. Her father reaches out to the ghost, traces a finger along the profile of a cheek.

"I'm expecting a baby, Dad."

He doesn't move, as if he hasn't heard or as if she spoke too softly to be heard from so far away, the place where he seems to have gone.

Irene makes an effort but, at the moment of telling him, she can't bring herself to say it, and something else seems more important.

"Who is she, Dad?"

ANNE MILANO APPEL, based in California, has translated works by a number of leading Italian authors for a variety of publishers in the US and UK. Her most recent translations include works by the award-winning Antonio Scurati and Paolo Maurensig. Her awards include the Italian Prose in Translation Award, the John Florio Prize for Italian Translation, and the Northern California Book Award for Translation.

Book Club Discussion Guides on our website.

World Editions promotes voices from around the globe by publishing books from many different countries and languages in English translation. Through our work, we aim to enhance dialogue between cultures, foster new connections, and open doors which may otherwise have remained closed.

Also available from World Editions:

The Performance
Claudia Petrucci
Translated from the Italian by Anne Milano Appel
"This unsettling and stunning tale explores the boundary between reality and illusion in the theater world."
—*Publishers Weekly*, starred review

A Devil Comes to Town
Paolo Maurensig
Translated from the Italian by Anne Milano Appel
"A masterfully constructed gothic horror story designed to keep aspiring writers up at night."
—*Kirkus Reviews*

Game of the Gods
Paolo Maurensig
Translated from the Italian by Anne Milano Appel
"An intriguing historical narrative of Indian chess master Malik Mir Sultan. Maurensig's tragic tale of genius and destiny duly salvages a forgotten hero."
—*Publishers Weekly*

The Cut Line
Carolina Pihelgas
Translated from the Estonian by Darcy Hurford
In the dog days of an Estonian summer, Liine flees to the countryside to put a conclusive end to her toxic fourteen-year relationship.

On the Design

As book design is an integral part of the reading experience, we would like to acknowledge the work of those who shaped the form in which the story is housed.

Tessa van der Waals (Netherlands) is responsible for the cover design, cover typography, and art direction of all World Editions books. She works in the internationally renowned tradition of Dutch Design. Her bright and powerful visual aesthetic maintains a harmony between image and typography, and captures the unique atmosphere of each book. She works closely with internationally celebrated photographers, artists, and letter designers. Her work has frequently been awarded prizes for Best Dutch Book Design.

The cover photo, entitled "Stairwell," was taken by Ingrid Michel in Frankfurt, on Goethe University's Campus Riedberg. "The light-flooded, circular staircase caught my eye and inspired me to take this photo. The skylight in the stairwell brings natural daylight into the interior of the modern building and opens up the view to the sky. The shot from a worm's-eye view emphasizes the spiral shape of the staircase. This creates a pull that draws the viewer into the picture."

Designer Tessa van der Waals selected the typeface for the title not only because of its name (LL Circular), but also because of its perfect round forms. The author's name is set in Eagle Bold, also a very circular typeface. Eagle Bold, a famous titling face, was originally designed by Morris Fuller Benton in 1933 for the National Recovery Administration and became the symbol of American recovery. It was restyled and digitized by David Berlow in the 1990s.

Euan Monaghan (United Kingdom) is responsible for the typography and careful interior book design.

The text on the inside covers and the press quotes are set in Circular, designed by Laurenz Brunner (Switzerland) and published by Swiss type foundry Lineto.

All World Editions books are set in the typeface Dolly, specifically designed for book typography. Dolly creates a warm page image perfect for an enjoyable reading experience. This typeface is designed by Underware, a European collective formed by Bas Jacobs (Netherlands), Akiem Helmling (Germany), and Sami Kortemäki (Finland). Underware are also the creators of the World Editions logo, which meets the design requirement that "a strong shape can always be drawn with a toe in the sand."

www.ingramcontent.com/pod-product-compliance
Lightning Source LLC
Jackson TN
JSHW021053010326
98696JS00004B/5

* 9 7 8 1 6 4 2 8 6 1 6 3 1 *